AF484259

ONE TRUE PURPOSE

THE EXTRAORDINARY LIFE OF A STUDENT AT MAGIC ACADEMY

- The Beginning -

CHARACTERS

Simon Anion
Water first-year

Marie Anion
Water second-year

Domizio
Guardian Spirit of Earth

Rachael Gennari
Water first-year

Lucas Gennari
Water first-year

Mark Solus
Water first-year

Phillip Fortus Royals
Earth third-year

Ferdinand Ascalis
Earth first-year

Faris Crest
Headmaster of Solset Academy

Tonio Frimo
Head doctor of Solset Academy

Table of Contents

Copyright

ONE TRUE PURPOSE VOLUME 1
CHRNOMAKER

Translated by: chrnomaker & teacup2also
Edited by: teacup2also
Cover art by: uiyoyo199
Illustrated by: uiyoyo199

Version 1.1: October 2022
ISBN: 9798836276591

001: Prologue (the Past)

Tears marked my face.

My bleeding body was covered in wounds, but it was my spirit that was being torn apart. Huddled in a corner of the room, I could do nothing but cry.

Why... Just why...

As I remained lost in my thoughts, a gentle light filtered into the gloomy room. Familiar footsteps approached me.

"There you are...you're all battered again!"

"Ah..."

Struggling to hold back my tears, I threw myself into the familiar girl's arms.

That gentle voice belonged to my older sister, Marie Anion. Though she was only eight years old, she had a surprisingly adult aura about her.

Her chestnut hair, which was long enough to reach her shoulders, shone in an otherworldly light that could illuminate all, even this somber room. Her hazelnut eyes gave a warm glow like two bright stars in this tiny, dark universe. Even though she was only a little taller than me, I felt tiny and insignificant before her radiance.

"Looks like those rascals never learn... Next time, I'll have to teach them a real lesson!"

I wanted to tell her it would be useless, but I could only sob and hold her tighter.

"There, there... Don't cry, Simon. You're already a young man, aren't you? And young men don't cry, now, do they?"

What, and girls can cry all they want?!

That's what I wanted to retort, but I held back my tears and nodded in silence. A kind warmth enveloped me.

"That's right! There you go... Dry your tears and raise your head. Your sister is here for you."

I finally stopped crying, but I didn't want to let go. My sister said nothing, stroking my head until I was finally calm again.

When I realized I was overindulging in her care, I let go of her arms with a start. She gave a slight chuckle.

"Look, I like caring for my little brother, okay?"

"…Shut up; you're barely a year older than me!"

"But you're still younger. Get over here and let me spoil you a little!" She opened her arms, welcoming me back. But now that I felt better, I tried to resist.

"Come on!"

"I'm fine now, so…"

"There's no need to pretend to be strong."

"…"

I finally stopped resisting and fell into my sister's arms once more. Her gentle touch slowly but surely eased my pain.

"I'm sorry…"

"…There's no need to apologize. It isn't your fault."

There was a reason why I had all these bruises. And this wasn't the first time.

All because I was different…

"It's not your fault that I'm—"

My sister stopped me with an all-encompassing hug.

"I will protect you, so stop dwelling on that. You are my little brother. I am here for you…"

My strength slowly faded away, and I completely entrusted the weight of my body to my sister's warm embrace.

This was eight years ago, and our story had barely begun.

002: Prologue (the Present)

In a certain landlocked kingdom in the upper center of a certain continent, where magic, magical creatures, and all kinds of non-human races existed, a certain building was oddly decorated for a not-so-odd event. Our story takes place in a certain institution at the center of this kingdom, near its most renowned lake. Its name?

Solset Magic Academy.

Surrounded by greenery, the academy did not suffer too much from the fall in temperature that marked the beginning of autumn. You could almost say that nothing was out of place, but…

"Hmm… It would seem that this year, too, there are many new students…"

"Well, it would be strange if there weren't."

"Do you know who your representative will be?"

"This year, *that* student is my favorite!"

"…"

Four fairies—red, blue, green, and yellow in color—and a brown lizard were arranged in a circle atop a marble table. Beneath them, a crystal skylight gave them a clear view of the auditorium below.

The new students inside it all attended the magic academy, which was in the middle of its opening ceremony. About three hundred fifteen-year-old students were seated in an orderly manner in that lavish building, in which large statues of even larger creatures were placed. All was silent, save the prominent voice of the elder that seemed to be the academy's headmaster.

Although the location of the five creatures made it seem like they were outdoors, a white dome shielded their bodies from the weather, and vines stretched everywhere except where the creatures rested. They could gaze at the people below from their lofty position above the auditorium's skylight, but the same could not be said of the students and staff in the auditorium.

Atop the marble table was a tray filled with cookies of many shapes, and in front of each creature, a cup of tea was carefully placed. Despite having been poured quite some time ago, the tea was still warm.

"Why do you bother to observe the new students? It has been quite some time since we last found any promising youths."

"Oh, but wouldn't it be wonderful if this year were the fateful year? I have a great feeling about this cohort!"

Questioned by the red fairy, who was quite strict, the yellow fairy responded cheerfully. The blue fairy then gave her opinion, calm as always:

"That's exactly what you said last year, I believe. And it ended just like the previous one..."

"It never hurts to check!"

It seemed that the yellow fairy was becoming a bit flustered.

"While we're at it, didn't you *just* say that you'd already found a favorite?"

"It still never hurts to take a look..."

This simple and direct query from the green fairy seemed to be the final nail in the coffin—the yellow fairy was now visibly panicking.

Even though there were no visual obstructions in between them, the fairies' figures were all blurry. No average person would be able to discern their true forms: they each appeared simply as a colored sphere with fairy wings. Oddly enough, however, the brown lizard's figure was fully visible.

"Despite what I said earlier, this year, our representatives have at least shown some promise!"

It seemed that the red fairy could use tones other than 'strict,' after all. Even the blue fairy spoke a few more words than usual:

"I agree. It's not often that our representatives show real promise, so even something like this is worthy of some celebration."

Nibbling on the cookies all the while, the four fairies continued their jovial discussion —they were clearly enjoying the occasion. The lizard, on the other hand...

"..."

...was as gloomy as always.

"Domizio, how many times do I have to tell you... It would do you well to accept the system."

The brown lizard, whose name was evidently Domizio, glared at the red fairy.

"Do I not already accept it the same as all of you? Leave me alone, Adamanta!"

"And yet, you're the only one who doesn't guide their representative properly."

Following Adamanta's riposte, the blue fairy tried to maintain the peace, but even she couldn't help but lightly chide Domizio:

"Now, now, everyone calm down... But Domizio, I've heard that you sometimes ignore your representative for the entire year."

"Shut up, Serena! I have my reasons."

With a sigh, the green fairy summed up the situation in just two words:

"Poor things…"

"Poor *them*? Where does that leave *me*, Breeze?"

Even the yellow fairy—Tiana—struggled to remain positive through all of this. Trying to understand Domizio's motivations, she aired her opinion:

"But this year, you seem even more frustrated than normal, you know?"

Domizio gave no response to Tiana's question. Curious, Serena decided to probe further:

"Does it by any chance have something to do with who's been chosen to be your academic representative for the year?"

Hearing this, Domizio glared even more threateningly. But Adamanta and Breeze were unfazed, and they took this opportunity to chime in:

"Give it up, Domizio. You know we've had years like that, too."

"And don't forget what happens to students who don't have a representative…"

They were at ease—the issue wasn't theirs to solve.

"Tch…"

Domizio distanced himself from the group, annoyed.

"…He never changes."

Hearing Adamanta's resignation, Tiana was quite curious:

"Since when was he like this?"

Rhetorical question or not, Breeze gave a serious response:

"I'd say since the representatives of his element began abusing their privilege while ignoring all of their responsibilities."

In a low voice, Serena added an obvious point:

"The only partner he ever trusted was *him*…"

"Yes, but then *that* happened…"

"And that's why Domizio was hurt."

Adamanta and Breeze sighed; neither could do anything but confirm it.

✳✳✳

While the four fairies talked about the past, Domizio moved away—leaving the dome—and walked toward the inside of the building, far from the auditorium.

Him, huh...

The only companion that Domizio had ever considered a true partner was already dead. Without a doubt, Domizio was hurt, but that wasn't the main reason why he was ignoring his responsibilities as a supervisor.

The main reason...it was as Breeze said. The behavior of the previous representatives of his element—Earth—had deteriorated.

In recent decades, believing that the role of representing Solset's Earth element was nothing more than an easy way to satisfy their ambitions, the Earth representatives had slowly forgotten the ancient honor that the title represented. In short, the whole element was in decline, and this year...was no different.

Hah... This year will be a bad one; I can feel it.

He had already resigned himself to his fate.

While the other four were having their discussion, he had investigated the new Earth students who had gathered for the opening ceremony, but no one was an ideal candidate for the position of representative. Morale at rock bottom, he made himself invisible with a spell and decided to wander through the building where the opening ceremony took place.

Although much smaller than the grand main building in which lectures were held, it was not small at all if you judged it by the standards of ordinary folk. On the contrary, at two stories (the dome wasn't included, because entry was restricted), it was comparable to the fancy villas of the middle nobility. Mainly used for official ceremonies of the academy, it was a stately place where students and professors were under the watchful eyes of the protectors—the five Guardian Spirits of the kingdom.

And one of those Guardian Spirits...was sighing.

This year will truly be a bad one...

Should I do as I did in previous years and simply leave my representative alone?

Lost in his thoughts, he aimlessly walked down one of the empty corridors of the building...or at least, that was how it seemed.

Hmm...?

In the distance, he could hear two anxious voices, one female and one male.

"Come on! You're already late!"

"And whose fault is that, Marie? I told you I could skip breakfast!"

"You shouldn't skip the first meal of the day, especially not on a day like this!"

The voices' owners were approaching Domizio. Soon, their shapes became more defined. The girl was wearing a second-year winter uniform, while the boy was wearing one for first-years.

Solset's uniform had a standard style for boys and girls, further divided into summer and winter uniforms. Both styles had long sleeves and an academic emblem on the left breast, but the male uniform was paired with a red jacket, whereas the female uniform was paired with a short red cape that just covered the shoulders. Complementing the vermilion base of the uniform shirt were golden tassels. Golden embroidery adorned the brown pants of the male uniform and the tights of the female uniform, a subtle sign of the academy's prestige.

There was no obligation to wear one style or the other. Since it was the middle of September, the weather continued to change, and the proportion of the students that wore their winter uniforms changed with it. Although the temperature was still relatively high, the occasional wind helped such early adopters cope with the heat.

The girl had chestnut hair that reached her elbows and hazel eyes that seemed to be overflowing with vitality. Her luxuriant hair was gathered in a large blue butterfly accessory, highlighting its sheer abundance.

The boy had chestnut hair, too, but his hair was all messy. Despite this, you could tell they were related by the unusual cowlick that they both shared. The boy's hazel eyes were also lively, but...

Both had the emblem of *Water*.

They're not my students, huh...

Indeed, Domizio's walk was *not* aimless: he was looking for students of his element that were as late as these two, on the off chance that they were worthy of being his representative. These two, however, were Serena's responsibility.

Magic was split into five major elements—Earth, Fire, Water, Wind, and Lightning—and each mage had an affinity for one of these. Because Solset was an elite academy of the Kingdom of Gilar, the academic staff couldn't waste time teaching the students spells that they would not be able to use to any great effect; thus, lessons were focused on each student's major element, and Domizio would have nothing to do with this sibling pair.

Determined not to obstruct the two, Domizio moved from the floor to the wall and continued walking down the corridor, passing by the pair in the process. He didn't even turn his gaze toward them and instead continued to sigh, hoping that at least some students of his element were similarly late.

"...Hmm?"

Suddenly, something outside one of the windows in the hallway caught his attention.

A creature was hovering just outside the building, perhaps thirty meters in the air. From its color and shape, it looked like a gargoyle—a resilient creature made from stone that was known as a guardian of wealthy and dangerous territories. One might question why there was one so close to the academy. More importantly, however...

How did it get past the surveillance?

Already in a bad mood, Domizio decided to hurl all of his irritation at this unwanted guest.

A magic circle formed just outside the window. The gargoyle seemed alarmed, but it was too late: in the blink of an eye, Domizio launched a magic bullet in its direction at supersonic speed, leaving it no time to react. Without even a cursory glance at the gargoyle, the lizard started walking once more.

I'll also have to talk to Faris about this... What an annoying day.

That moment of distraction almost proved fatal.

The depressing atmosphere that surrounded Domizio instantly disappeared. He snapped to attention, having perceived a tremendous amount of magical power. The gargoyle that had supposedly been shot down began to pick up speed, heading in the direction of the opening ceremony.

Impossible! A magical creature should disappear after taking that much damage! Perhaps...

His moment of distraction may have denied him the chance for a timely response, but he wasn't worried in the slightest. They were inside the academy, where an impenetrable magical barrier was established. At worst, the gargoyle might create a bit of a commotion among the students and a headache for the headmaster, who would have to find an excuse for it.

Because of this lackadaisical attitude, the lizard did not notice what then occurred behind him.

A magical cluster darted past Domizio and shattered the window, thoroughly intent on piercing that gargoyle. The practically simultaneous sounds of glass shattering and the creature crumbling to pieces overlapped and reverberated through the air.

What happened?!

The lizard turned around to find the same two students standing still, looking at the broken window. No... One of the students had their gaze turned in another direction.

"Finish your work properly next time."

Hearing those words of reprimand, the lizard was sure that he had been spotted.

How is that possible?! Surely I'm still invisible!

"Simon, what happened?"

"Nothing much. Some debris was about to fall on us."

"Oh, I see."

The female student seemed to easily accept the male student's answer; the Guardian Spirit was nonplussed. But before he could even open his mouth to question the pair, the girl urged the boy to move.

"The ceremony! We'd better run!"

"No need to say it twice!"

Missing the opportunity to reveal himself, the lizard could only watch as the two students ran off.

"Marie, does the academy's defense system consist of lizard-like magical creatures?"

"Hmm… I haven't heard of anything like that, but the Guardian Spirit of Earth is said to be a lizard. I've never seen him personally, though."

Without any further words, the two disappeared around the corner.

Only Domizio remained in the hallway, stunned. His invisibility spell faded away, but he did not seem to notice or care.

"How…?"

The fact that he was seen, the fact that the boy destroyed the academy's magic barrier from the inside… But most importantly…

Why did his magic seem so familiar…?

At that moment, a fire was lit inside Domizio. He grinned from ear to ear.

"…I've found him…"

Eyes burning with ardor, he tried to remember the boy's name.

"Simon…"

Nothing about him stood out, but he caught the lizard's curiosity all the same—a curiosity that hadn't been stirred for decades.

He will be the representative of my element for years to come.

003: The Beginning I

"…And thus, I wish you all a good academic year!"

At the end of the headmaster's speech, we first-year students were to gather in our classes.

"See you later, Simon. When you come back, this time I'll be the one making you lunch."

"Don't burn anything like last time!"

"Don't worry; I won't!"

With that foreboding statement, my sister headed home. The second- and third-year students all had today off, since the first day of the academic year was dedicated entirely to new arrivals.

Each element was divided into three academic years, which were further divided into two classes of about thirty students. Since only the elite students of the kingdom gathered in Solset, there were rarely more than three hundred new students per year. It was a brutal competition; merely qualifying for the academy spoke volumes about one's magical ability.

Each student was recognized by the emblem on the left breast of their academy uniform; these emblems were decorated in the color that represented the student's elemental specialty. Red was Fire, blue was Water, green was Wind, yellow was Lightning, and brown was Earth.

First-year emblems were a simple diamond shape, while second-year emblems included an additional ribbon-like ornament. Drawn on the emblems of third-year Fire, Water, Wind, and Lightning students was a fairy; those of Earth instead featured a lizard. Although the majority of those who possessed a fairy emblem were girls and most with a lizard emblem were boys, it was simply a matter of natural aptitude; the former made greater use of the magical arts—which required complex techniques to cast—while the latter made use of both magic and physical might.

My emblem was a simple blue diamond shape, but my sister's, though also blue, was more ornate; we were of the same element, but she was a year older than me.

After being assigned to a class, I waited for the professor to arrive. I took a look around, and there were exactly thirty students including me; unsurprisingly, since I was in a more magic-oriented element, most of my classmates were female.

Just as I was about to take a closer look, the door opened, and the students' murmurs stopped. It was our professor, a very kind-looking gentleman in his forties.

He didn't immediately commence the academic program, instead asking everyone to introduce themselves; this took up what little time was left of the class after the entrance ceremony.

After a brief introduction from everyone and a bell that announced the morning break, the class was alive with chatter.

Who knows how long it's been...

Smiling faintly, I noticed that two boys had approached me.

"Hey there, how's it going?"

"You seem lost in thought. I hope you don't mind if we disturb you?"

My smile became more visible.

"Not at all, um…"

"Lucas Gennari. And this is Mark Solus."

"Simon Anion. Pleased to meet you!"

""The pleasure is ours.""

And that's how I made my first friends in the academy.

The lively boy in the summer uniform who had silver hair, scarlet eyes, and an almost bewitching voice was Lucas, while the more reserved boy in the winter uniform with chestnut hair, emerald eyes, and a calm aura exuding from him was Mark. Lucas wore gloves that covered only his thumbs and index fingers, whereas Mark—instead of wearing a tie—kept a cross-shaped pendant on his neck and wore a ceremonial stole under the collar of his uniform. He also wore bracelets on his wrists that looked like they were made of brambles.

"So you're not from this kingdom, Simon?"

"No, I'm from Serfia, the kingdom that borders with Patania and Lunia."

Serfia was located northwest of Gilar, the kingdom to which this academy belonged. To reach Serfia by the most direct route, one first had to pass through Patania.

"In your self-introduction, you said you also have a sister. Is she from Serfia too?"

"Yes, we moved here two years ago. In the first year, we settled down a bit, and in the second year, my sister started to attend this academy. Back then, my health was quite poor, but I got better and enrolled at the academy this year."

Lucas and Mark were barraging me with questions, but I answered them all calmly. There was nothing to worry about. Here, at least, I didn't have to worry about my identity. After two years of *seemingly* laid-back life, such an ordinary conversation would not be able to expose me.

"So you have a weak constitution?"

Mark's question was thoughtful, of a completely different kind to what I experienced years ago.

"Far from it. The truth is…I'm not very skilled at magical arts."

Lucas and Mark were astonished, and their surprise was understandable. This was Solset, the kingdom's most prestigious magical academy. After graduating here, the only common career paths were magical researcher…or soldier.

I continued with my explanation:

"My magical affinity isn't great, and I can barely perform certain spells; I've had to work very hard to reach the minimum standards of the academy. That I was able to make it at all—is thanks to my sister. I really owe her a lot…"

Hearing my words, Lucas made a joke:

"Someone *really* loves his sister, eh?"

"That is absolutely correct."

At my immediate response, their jaws dropped.

After an embarrassing pause, I giggled. A few seconds later, the two of them started giggling too.

"To say that with such a straight face… You really caught me off guard!"

"Your sister's name is Marie, right? And she's a second-year at this academy?"

"Yes, that's right."

Thinking that my earlier statement wasn't serious, they ignored it. I didn't really mind, though, so I didn't bother correcting them. It was, however, a good time to ask them a question of my own:

"Do you happen to know her?"

The two of them looked each other in the eye and turned their heads toward a particular group of girls.

"Rachael, we need your help!"

Reluctantly, a girl—Rachael, presumably—with long silver hair and scarlet eyes approached us. An aura of pure annoyance suffused the room with every step that she took; she was clearly displeased to have been called out while she was in the process of making new friends.

Despite this, Lucas asked a question:

"Do you happen to know Marie Anion? This guy here is concerned about the public image of his *dearest* sister!"

Seemingly wiping invisible sweat from his forehead, he winked at the girl and added a 'Please…'

Rachael sighed.

"You should really stop relying on me and start finding things out for yourself, you know?"

Having said these words, she looked back at me.

"So, you're Marie's brother?"

Puzzled, I shyly asked Rachael a question:

"Um… Do you maybe know my sister?"

Gesturing as if she were touching the side of an invisible pair of glasses, she triumphantly announced:

"But of course! Such information is nothing for everyone's favorite secret informant— yours truly!"

"…"

*My common sense may be a bit off, but…*secret *informant? A dazzling girl like her?*

I didn't vocalize that thought, though.

"What can you tell me about her?"

Grimacing, she outright refused me:

"Why should I share the information I *personally* gathered with someone like you?"

Unsure how to answer that, I resorted to my ace in the hole.

I put my hands together…

…lowered my head…

…and exaggeratedly raised my voice.

"Please, O Great Secret Informant!"

I shouted my request for the whole class to hear.

Flabbergasted, Rachael didn't answer immediately, but after realizing that all eyes were on her, she gave a sigh of resignation.

"Uh… I was joking, you know? There's no need to be so desperate! Also, what kind of secret informant would I be if I didn't have any clients?"

Seemingly making excuses, she couldn't hide the hint of nervousness in her voice. I gave her a small apology in my mind.

"Hah… You're really, *really* obsessed with your sister, huh…"

"Sure am!"

At my straightforward answer, Rachael froze. After a beat, Lucas broke the ice with a pat on her shoulder.

"There's a new one in town!"

"Shut it, you weirdo!"

"Hey, what's wrong with caring about your own sister? …Now that I think about it, that uniform looks positively stunning on you… What do you say, Simon?"

At Lucas's invitation, I gave Rachael's clothing a once-over.

She was wearing her summer uniform—which had shorter socks and sleeves than the winter uniform—but she also wore the short red cape of her winter uniform. Maybe it was to protect her from the cold wind? I wasn't sure if it was because of the cold or for fashion, but she was wearing gloves that, unlike Lucas's ones, entirely covered her hands.

Adorning her silvery hair were two black barrettes that together held a single lock of hair in place. Atop her head was a slightly puffy hat that proudly displayed a pin of a mascot that had recently become popular in the kingdom. Synthetic feathers decorated her hat, giving her an adventurer-like image; meanwhile, the small bag that hung from the belt around her waist reinforced the informant-like image that she was trying to display, and her black cross-shaped earrings topped off her somewhat mischievous demeanor.

The white shirt she wore highlighted her modest curves, while her black stockings came to just the right height to form the infamous 'absolute territory'; one's gaze couldn't help but flit between the stockings and the skirt while paying no less attention to the sight of those pillowy thighs. You could also catch a glimpse of the hooks of her garter belt, which spoke of her particular taste in fashion—I was sure that this captivated the attention of quite a few male students in the class…not that there were many to begin with.

I could have sworn that the skirt on the girls' uniform were longer, but…I had a feeling I shouldn't say this out loud.

All in all, there was only one possible conclusion I could come to:

"I don't know how she looked before, but this uniform definitely suits her very well."

Visibly blushing, Rachael tried to flee. However, after turning around and seeing all eyes on her, she turned back to face Lucas with a frustrated look on her face and started bickering with him.

In the meantime, I tilted my body slightly toward Mark.

"Listen… Are Lucas and Rachael siblings?"

Sorry to put you in the spotlight, but I really want to know more about my sister.

This question came naturally to my mind from the snippets of their argument that I could hear.

"Yes. Although they don't seem to get along, Lucas cares very much for his younger sister. Rachael doesn't deny any favor requested by him, either."

"They're pretty close, huh…"

Envying them, I watched the siblings' squabble from a moderate distance.

Looking at me from the side, Mark closed his eyes, touched the cross on his neck, and murmured something under his breath. When he finished, I asked him what he was doing:

"Is there something you wanted to tell me?"

"Oh, it's nothing much; you can think of it as a prayer. Anyway, we'd better stop them before they cause too much trouble. Just look what they're doing!"

Rachael was throwing chairs, while Lucas was hiding behind a makeshift fort made of desks.

"I'd say they've gone far enough already!"

I got up from my desk to stop the two of them. When I stepped away, I heard Mark's faint voice:

"I hope you and your sister get along well, too…"

***

Only the ringing of the bell managed to calm the mess caused by those two, and the professor's arrival was at last able to produce a temporary truce.

After a brief explanation of the various procedures to be followed within the academy and a general introduction to the geopolitical situation, we were reminded that although we were simple students, we had a duty to take control of the situation and help civilians evacuate in the event of an enemy invasion.

No one paid much attention to this warning, though.

The Kingdom of Gilar was not so wide as to cover a large portion of the continent, but it had always maintained a policy of non-aggression and was protected by the five Guardian Spirits. Even in the unlikely event of an invasion from the nearest border, it would still take at least four days at maximum speed for an enemy force to reach the academy.

For this reason, the students' attitudes were not tense at all. The professor clearly displayed some internal conflict over this lack of tension but also relief at seeing his students smile like that.

Since it was the first day, we were free from school duties at lunchtime. Before we left, the professor reminded us that in a few days he would announce something that would involve the entire class.

"I'm off!"

"Hey, wait up!"

Lucas ran out of the classroom in a hurry; Rachael chased after him. She probably wanted to resume their 'discussion' (squabble) from earlier.

Mark approached me.

"We're going to get lunch; Lucas is trying to get a seat in the dining hall."

I wanted to ask him why Rachael was running like that too, but maybe it was some sibling competition that I couldn't comprehend. I envied their relationship...

Seemingly sensing my melancholy, Mark tried to cheer me up:

"Would you like to join us?"

His invitation was warm, and his smile showed no malice—completely different from what I had experienced before.

It's...radiant...

Suddenly, I remembered *that* situation. I shook my head to clear my thoughts.

He's not like them.

However, I could not accept his invitation.

"Sorry, Mark. I already have plans for lunch."

I stood up from my seat.

"I have someone waiting for me at home."

Seemingly understanding the meaning of my sentence, he did not try to persuade me.

"In that case, have a good lunch!"

He exited the room, and a little later, I did as well. Before I headed home, I turned to gaze at the empty classroom.

This will be my academic life.

No one noticed—perhaps not even me—but there was an expression of happiness on my face that I hadn't displayed in a very long time.

✳✳✳

Exhausted from the first day of class, I walked home.

Usually, students enrolled at the academy had their own apartment within the academy grounds, in order to make their stay more comfortable and convenient. These apartments were located in buildings divided not by gender but by element; as such, both male and female students lived together under the same roof.

My sister and I were an even more special case, however.

Ignoring the nearby Water dormitory, I headed toward the outer perimeter of the grounds. As I gradually walked up the hill, I slowly moved further and further away. After thirty minutes of walking, I caught a glimpse of my destination: the staff dormitory.

With such a vast campus and so many buildings to maintain, it was no wonder that this dormitory was larger than all of the student dormitories combined. Despite this, it was much simpler, with little originality; rather than students or professors, the staff who kept the academy running smoothly behind the scenes resided here.

Heading upstairs, I noticed something.

This time, I'm the one...

I opened the door to my apartment and was greeted by a sweet smell that stimulated my hunger...and my sister.

"Welcome back!"

Wearing a cute apron over her uniform and with her hair tied up in a ponytail, she waved at me.

Smiling from the bottom of my heart, I greeted her simply:

"I'm home!"

This time, I'm the one returning home.

Seated opposite me, my sister asked me about my day while showing off the lunch that she had prepared.

"It was all right. I've already made some friends, in fact."

I tasted the soup, not immediately noticing the grin that spread across her face.

"...What is it?"

"Nothing. I'm glad you found some friends after all this time."

I sipped at that bland soup once more. This time, however, my cheeks were slightly red.

It was about twice the size of a standard apartment, but although the table in the living room was clearly meant for four people, the bunk bed in the bedroom could hold only two. It was very likely that this apartment was originally two separate ones and had been remodeled to meet the needs of the residents.

Even after using a certain connection, my dear sister had had to try her very best to get this place where we could live together. In the first year after we arrived in Gilar, she had worked so hard to collect as much money as possible for our living expenses. In the second year, she had dedicated herself to obtaining a scholarship to facilitate my enrollment; every year, the academy chose the highest-ranking students from the first and second years and exempted them from the annual tuition fee as a reward for their excellent grades.

I was against enrolling myself, but my sister didn't want to hear any excuses. Eventually, I gave in, but I adamantly declared that I would raise the amount needed to enroll on my own efforts. During the second year, I did everything I could to give my sister as little trouble as possible, from part-time jobs to housework, all to make her life easier while she was trying to get the scholarship.

Once she achieved the scholarship, my sister insisted that she had to start doing her share of the housework, but when I finally acquiesced, she was, for want of a better word…useless. After burning countless dishes, setting fire to a myriad of clothes while she tried to iron them, and once even flooding the apartment with soap while she was doing the laundry, she reluctantly conceded that I should do most of the housework, under the condition that I would teach her as I went. Little by little, and with some additional help from a few neighbors who knew about our financial situation, she started to improve.

"How's lunch today?"

"Bland as usual."

As I continued to sip at the soup, my sister gazed at me happily. Today, she truly gave her all for lunch. Even though it was all flavorless, I almost felt like I could taste the care with which she had prepared it. We talked about various things for the rest of the meal, including my new friends and what we would do next.

"Next week, representatives from every element of the academy will be appointed. Last year, it was an amazing event!"

One week after the opening ceremony, the highly anticipated appointment of new academic representatives would take place. From what Rachael and my sister told me, the representatives were the best students in their element and were responsible for many things, ranging from organizing events at the academy to maintaining public order.

After moving from Serfia, we had, with some difficulty, acquired this apartment, which was normally assigned to the academy staff.

This last point was fundamental: in recent years, an almost worldwide war had broken out. Serfia and Patania had been at war for a long time, and Lunia had just entered the fray. As for Gilar… Even though the kingdom was staunchly neutral and had declared as such, that was not enough to stop it from being the target of espionage and sabotage attempts.

Solset's academic representatives held great prestige and were appointed by the five Guardian Spirits, who had fought long ago against Kinlarus, the Demon King. After restoring peace, the Guardian Spirits had decided to watch over the coming generations, but they would not move for troubles caused by mere humans. As a result, although Gilar had no reason to go to war, it couldn't lower its guard, either.

"Do you think you'll be selected as the next Water representative?"

"Who do you think I am? Even though I got a scholarship, I'm not *that* good."

"And yet I was told that only two girls in your element are your equals, and one of them just graduated?"

With an embarrassed expression, my sister had no choice but to confess:

"It's not that I'm understating my abilities; it's just… A first- or second-year has never been an academic representative."

"You'll just have to be the first, then."

"No, if anything, I'd say *you*…"

My sister gave an apologetic look and quickly shut her mouth.

"Sorry, Simon…"

In response to her apology, I squeezed my hands on top of each other and bit my lip.

"No need to apologize. Look, I know I'm different from the rest, but I'm making an effort not to stand out. I've practiced a lot for this; you know that better than anyone, right?"

I slowly met her gaze.

"And I know how hard you've been working all this time."

"Simon…"

The tense atmosphere returned to normal. My sister gave a sigh of relief and continued:

"Anyway, the other girl is much more skilled than me. Even though I've been training with you forever, I don't think I could beat her in a fair fight."

For my sister to talk about someone else like that…she must really respect her.

"I understand… So the representatives are already decided?"

"More or less. The third-year graduates always have a disciple who then succeeds them after a year. I doubt it'll be any different this year!"

"Huh… So does that mean the 'appointment' is nothing but a sham, and the position is simply handed over to the current representative's lackey?"

My sister could only nod bitterly in response to this. After a short pause, I continued:

"Because of the war, all security is now undertaken by the academy staff, and thus, the representatives are merely tasked with helping the headmaster decide how to run certain events throughout the year. You could almost say that it's a role where you're praised for nothing but the work of others."

"Maybe you're right… You know, I've been thinking about this for a while, but how exactly do you know all of this?"

"Why, because of everyone's favorite secret informant, of course!"

Hearing me joke like this, my sister giggled gently and shed a happy tear.

"It looks like life at the academy is going very well for you so far…"

My sister was always worrying about me, and I wanted to do everything to burden her as little as possible, so I was glad to hear this.

"So… what about *your* friends, Marie? Will you finally start accepting their invitations?"

"Um… Maybe it *is* time, after all."

I breathed a sigh of relief.

Last year, my sister was always busy studying, and although I did the housework, she hardly had any leisure time. I was glad that she would finally be able to relax and enjoy her academic life.

"Sorry if I made you worry."

"Don't worry about it. Although, I do have another concern…"

"What is it?"

At my sister's invitation, I brought up the matter that had been weighing on me ever since I heard what Rachael said:

"About Phillip Royals, the candidate to represent Earth…"

"Hah…"

My sister could only sigh, unable to hide her surprise.

"I'd like to have a *little* chat with this secret informant of yours…"

"My apologies, but secret informants must remain *secret* informants."

Preventing her from changing the subject, I pressed on:

"I've heard that this Phillip is courting you."

Forget embarrassed—my sister just looked tired.

"Yes, for at least half a year now. He keeps blabbering on about my beauty, elegance, and so on, but I'm sure he's not sincere."

At this, I clenched my fist tightly around my fork.

"Do you want me to…*take care of him*?"

"Please stop! There's no need for that!"

I released the fork and continued eating normally.

Panicking at my joke (it seemed that she thought I was serious), she continued with her explanation:

"At the beginning of the year, he was clearly suspicious of me for my questionable social background, but when I started getting results, he suddenly started talking to me quite regularly. He clearly doesn't mean well, but he hasn't done anything to me yet, so there's nothing to worry about for now."

I was relieved to hear that.

"If he ever harasses you, let me know."

My sister's eyes wavered, so I repeated myself more firmly:

"You absolutely must tell me. Promise?"

I couldn't tell whether my gaze was full of murderous intent or concern, but my sister rose from her seat and approached me from behind. She embraced my back, and I could soon feel her gentle heartbeat.

"I promise you. So please don't have that look in your eyes…"

Despite my sister's pampering, I still couldn't stay calm.

"And if *you* have any problems, please don't hesitate to confide in me."

Whenever I got like this, she really tried to act like a big sister. To that request, however, I could not give a sincere affirmative response.

Staying silent, I awaited the next day.

004: The Appointment

A week had passed since the beginning of the academic year, and it was finally time for the fateful appointment of the academic representatives. No classes were scheduled for today, and the ceremony would begin one hour after the usual start of lessons. However, all students were already gathered in front of the academy. This behavior was not a demonstration of their diligence, though; rather, the students were simply excited—far from a boring formality, the appointment ceremony was practically a festival.

The parade would commence with a march by the Earth students, followed by an aerial performance by the Wind students. Concurrently, there would be a fireworks display run by the Fire students, while the Water students had the role of broadcasting the ceremony. Last, but certainly not least, the Lightning students supported the other specialties, coordinating the whole event.

The new students all crowded in the front square of the academy and fervently watched the second-years' opening display. Although the performances could hardly be described as 'spectacular,' they enthralled the eager first-years. Additionally, this opening display kept the new students away from those who were busy with ceremony preparations and heightened their expectations for what was to come. As one would expect, many performances involved the use of magic; however, there were also impressive displays of brawn, athleticism, and even stand-up comedy.

"Wow...the atmosphere is electrifying!"

Between couples, trios, and sometimes even groups of all five elements, the cheers of the spectators seemed like they would never fade. Observing all of this from the terrace of my apartment building, I could not complain about the view; although I was about two kilometers away, the aerial perspective gave me an excellent panorama of the enthusiastic displays and equally enthusiastic audience.

As I admired the festivities, a question happened to arise in my mind:

"...I wonder what my sister is doing?"

Since my sister was effectively the second-best of her element, she acted as a student liaison. She had been at work since a few hours ago, and unfortunately, first-years were not permitted to assist with this ceremony. As such, I was home alone; large crowds didn't really suit me, so I preferred to stay out of the way.

"...I still can't stand having too many eyes on me..."

In truth, being around too many people made me feel ill at ease. The feeling was mild in class, but simply setting foot in the dining hall or auditorium was enough to make me break out in a cold sweat.

The gazes may not have been directed toward me—but I felt uncomfortable nonetheless.

"And the appointment ceremony is in that very room…"

Just the thought of being in such a crowded place made me shudder…but that was not what currently occupied my mind.

"Phillip Royals…"

Last week, I acquired some more information about him: part of a noble family, his full name was Phillip Fortus Royals. Since the academy was a meritocracy, the flaunting of a noble name was heavily frowned upon and considered a sign of weakness. In fact, 'facts speak louder than prejudices' was practically a motto of the academy. All the academic achievements and family prestige in the world meant nothing during a true battle—that's why the academy rewarded results with such vigor.

Even so, it seemed that Phillip exhibited respectable magical ability and exceptional leadership; all of the magical-creature-suppression missions he had been involved in were always completed without mistakes. He was extremely charismatic, for that matter.

However…

"What a womanizer…"

The list of girls, of all elements, whom he was courting was practically uncountable— and included my own sister. He already had several girls working under him, but, despite this, his popularity was strangely high; there didn't seem to be any Earth students who criticized him in any meaningful capacity. I had a suspicion that there were negotiations taking place behind the scenes, but I elected not to pry further.

I had already obtained all the information I needed: he was someone to avoid at all costs.

And if he dares to try anything with my sister—

The thundering *boom* of a pyrotechnic shot resounded through the sky, snapping me out of my thoughts.

"It's about to begin, huh…"

I decided to get going.

The building where my sister and I lived was located on a gentle hill, so a straight shot to the academic establishment was impossible. The necessary detour meant that it would take me almost thirty minutes to reach my destination, but I could still take my time—the appointment ceremony would commence an hour after the start of the festival.

I saw few people on my route, as nearly everyone was watching the students' performances live. In fact, the only people I met along the way were academy employees.

Most of them were ordinary people who had accepted job offers posted on the bulletin board at the nearest city (about thirty minutes away by carriage), but there were also former academy students who, in order to avoid joining the military, decided to stay on at the academy and assist the professors.

Not too far from my dormitory, I saw the first screens displaying the student performances. Composed of fine water droplets, these screens reflected light from various mirrors placed at key points throughout the academy and allowed people who were not on-site to visually observe the exhibitions as if they were directly in front of them. Although no audio was available—for reasons that I will not go into, the Water students rarely cooperated on the exhibition broadcasts with the Wind students, who usually handled audio—the crowd was so loud that this wasn't an issue.

The academy's broadcast system was quite versatile, and it could even be used for more critical events, in which formality and utmost precision were required; such cases were usually VIP receptions, duels between well-known students in the academy arena, or enemy attack. The transmission coverage was able to reach the entire academy grounds thanks to the Guardian Spirits, whose cooperation also allowed a highly secure transmission with no risk of enemy interception.

Similar broadcasts were rare outside the academy grounds and were limited to a one-kilometer radius. This radius was not a hard limit, though; magic concatenation could be used to further extend the transmission range, but this would result in the signal being more easily disturbed and intercepted. Indeed, one could say that the Guardian Spirits' cooperation made Solset the safest area in the entire kingdom.

That said, their presence also resulted in the academy having the highest density and variety of magical creatures: such creatures were born from magical noise suffusing the air, and there was a particularly high density of such noise in areas of the academy where more than one Guardian Spirit's magical protection overlapped and interfered.

Although many of these magical creatures were born naturally, they could at times also be artificially induced. And the most dangerous of these beings...

...were demons.

Just after I finished this train of thought, I felt an abnormal stagnation in the air.

This—was a familiar feeling.

It can't be... How can there be one so close to the academy?!

The appointment ceremony was about to begin, but I couldn't turn a blind eye to such grave danger. Somewhat reluctantly, I decided to quickly confirm the extent of the magical anomaly. After all...

It might be my fault.

✳✳✳

"Damn it! At this rate, I'm going to be late!"

I had gotten pretty close to the anomaly. For the moment, it didn't seem to warrant great caution, but it would definitely be worth keeping an eye on over the coming days. I was sure that, even if I let it go, it would soon disappear on its own. Most importantly, however…

It isn't my fault.

I wanted to sigh with relief, but I was currently breathing too hard. At this rate, I would definitely be as late as I'd been on the first day, but I ran as fast as I could to reach the auditorium even a second faster.

When I got to the plaza, there was no one outside the building. Everyone was no doubt inside, listening to the appointment of the new representatives.

I hurried upstairs, trying to make as little noise as possible, and soon arrived in front of the hall. As on the first day, the doors were open, but since this was an event for all students—unlike the opening ceremony—many students were crowded outside. Because of this, no one noticed my arrival, and I was able to blend in with the crowd.

It seemed that the Fire, Water, Wind, and Lightning representatives had already been nominated. Four female third-year students—each with a different elemental emblem on their chest—stood at a moderate distance from each other, in front of the banner representing their elemental specialty. I couldn't see their respective Guardian Spirits.

From what my sister told me, it seemed that except in emergencies, each Guardian Spirit only showed themselves to their element's academic representative and others whom they respected. As such, they wouldn't appear before such a crowd. It seemed like I was still just in time to see the announcement of the Earth representative.

I finally caught my breath. I was very much not looking forward to seeing *that* person being appointed as representative, so I was considering going back…but the students' astonishment made me change my mind. Some kind of brown iguana, perhaps a meter long, appeared atop the lectern that was in front of the Earth banner.

The dorsal crests that ran down his entire back and tail scattered the light like amber, but the fluid movements that he executed gave no indication of rigidity. From his half-closed jaws, one could glimpse countless fangs that were uncharacteristic of such a reptile, reaffirming his imposing figure. A vacant gaze ambled through the audience, making the students more anxious by the second.

It's…!

There was no doubt about it. This was the same lizard.

The one I saw on my first day at school.

I…had a bad feeling about this.

"My name is Domizio, and I am the Guardian Spirit of Earth.

"I will now proceed to nominate my representative. The next representative of Earth—"

The lizard quickly scanned the crowd, not giving the astonished students any time to compose themselves.

His gaze forcibly crossed mine.

"—will be Simon Anion, first-year of Water!"

***

"Just what is the meaning of this?!"

A cry of outrage echoed throughout the room as a male student stood up with a clatter. His blond hair was pulled back into a pigtail that spilled over the back of his rebelliously worn summer uniform, and an irrepressible rage radiated from his crimson eyes.

Phillip Royals was visibly indignant.

"It is exactly as I said."

A brown lizard stood on the stage and spoke through some kind of microphone that was used to announce the new representatives. The students' eyes were divided between the two of them…

…and me.

"Simon Anion, first-year of Water, will be the next representative of Earth."

"That doesn't make any sense!"

Most students, of Earth or otherwise, shared Phillip's dissent.

"Why should a new student take responsibility as an academic representative when he's not even from the same element? An element's representative should belong to the element itself; that's just common sense!"

A loud voice of rejection echoed through the hall. The only calm 'person' was that brown reptile.

"Am I to presume that you think *you* are qualified to be the representative?"

The hall fell silent.

After hesitating for a second and a brief stutter, Phillip soon regained his swagger:

"Y-yes, of course! I've already learned all the tasks I'll have to take on from last year's Earth representative. I'm first in all practical fields and can lead a team better than anyone. You'll find no better candidate than me!"

The lizard couldn't help but give a heavy sigh.

"And that…is exactly why you are not suitable."

"Wha…?"

"As a matter of fact, last year's representative and the one before that… No, it has been decades since there was someone who was truly suited for the role."

The students' murmurs swelled into a clamor.

It was no wonder—one of the Guardian Spirits of the kingdom was denigrating the representatives he had chosen, all of whom everyone respected greatly.

Four colored fairies whose figures were difficult to discern appeared and approached the reptile.

"Domizio, don't you think you might be exaggerating a little?"

"I second that. We get that you're frustrated, but—"

"That is exactly why I won't let this year end the same way as all the others."

The blue and green fairies tried to reason with the brown lizard, but it was no use.

"Simon Anion…I want you to be the representative of my element."

In the end, everyone's eyes turned to me, on the opposite side of the hall. I saw astonished, surprised, and even envious looks, but by far the most common were resentful stares.

The most intense one came from Phillip.

"This…is unacceptable!"

Making another attempt to strengthen his argument, he tried to reason with the Guardian Spirit without success. Crushed by the pressure of everyone's eyes, I raised my hand weakly.

"Um… Could I say something?"

Everyone stopped talking. Their focus was entirely on me.

"Go ahead."

That unusual brown lizard permitted me to speak.

I took a big breath and, accepting one of the microphones that had been handed to me, I spoke with some hesitation:

"Um… I decline the offer."

Chaotic murmurs resounded through the hall once more.

"Silence!"

At this single word from the Guardian Spirit, everyone fell silent with no hesitation; not even Phillip dared move.

"Unfortunately, this appointment cannot be revoked even by the student themselves. If you want to resign, you must leave the academy—or die."

"Wha…"

What kind of choices are those?!

…That's what I wanted to answer, but I kept quiet. Leaving the academy was a fine choice, but I certainly couldn't do so after all my sister had done to get me enrolled. As for the second…

I couldn't. At least, not now.

I took a moment to reflect, and then I resumed my argument:

"…Isn't it absurd that I should represent an element that isn't even my strongest?"

My first argument was Phillip's, which he had rightly brought up.

"The representative is theoretically the most charismatic and influential person of their element, to say nothing of the extreme mastery that they should have of spells. I am a new student who knows neither the duties nor the responsibilities of this role, and my magical mastery is hardly worthy of the representative position!"

'He's right!' and similar comments could be heard throughout the hall; the whispers swarmed in a rising wave.

The lizard responded:

"Naturally, the representative should possess all of the qualities that you mentioned, but that only applies under normal circumstances…"

I could practically *feel* the combined weight of everyone's curiosity.

"…This—is not a normal circumstance."

I didn't know why, but I got the impression that he was snickering.

"Every Guardian Spirit has the right to appoint the representative of their element without needing to take into consideration the opinions of others. Neither the professors nor even the other Guardian Spirits can go against their appointment."

That's absurd!

The students started discussing among themselves how dictatorial this system was. Still, no one dared to say it louder than a conspiratorial whisper. After all, pointing this out would mean rebuking the Guardian Spirit, who had helped defeat the Demon King.

I took another sigh before resuming my case:

"...But that means going against the will of the students themselves. Under these circumstances, the elected representative would surely be targeted by those who are against their appointment."

"That is of no concern to me."

Leaving me dumbfounded, the brown lizard resumed his explanation:

"What the elected representative must do in order to prove their worthiness is very simple: they must survive all the harassment of those who are against them. Otherwise, their choices are as before—leave, or die."

Without giving me any time to respond, the lizard added:

"Do you really think that we would be so stubborn as to choose a representative who could be eliminated by mere students?"

That phrasing was definitely unexpected... Could he know my true strength?

Everyone seemed to stare at me with an air of admiration or terror.

Not this feeling again...

Resisting the urge to throw up, I hesitatingly gave voice to my last resort:

"...And the vote of no confidence?"

"...Oh?"

When he heard that argument, the lizard's gaze focused entirely on me. Most of the other students were quite puzzled, and some were even asking their neighbors what I was talking about.

In the end, all eyes focused on me. I proceeded with the explanation:

"The vote of no confidence is a complaint from most of the students involved in a given matter. This complaint can be only accepted if eighty percent or more of the students involved do not accept the current situation, and it cannot be revoked by anyone—not even a Guardian Spirit."

The murmurs rippled uncontrollably throughout the hall once more.

"Where did you get this information?"

"In the academy's rulebook, of course. Is it really that much of a surprise?"

Concerned about many things, I had read the rules several times to find loopholes that seemed like they might in any way be useful...but I never expected to use one right at the beginning of the year!

However, rather than panicking, the lizard practically seemed to smile.

"As you say, the vote of no confidence cannot be revoked, not even by a Guardian Spirit..."

"Then...!"

Surely, more than eighty percent of the students of Earth—no, of the entire academy—were against my nomination.

"...but are you really sure that you want to do this? That you want to revoke *my order*, dear students?"

All students were paralyzed by his words.

Of course, if the vote of no confidence were approved and a new representative were chosen, the students would be happy, but...it would incite the wrath of a Guardian Spirit. Whoever the new representative was, they would be unable to lead a comfortable academic life even if they wished for it, and neither would the students who were against the Guardian Spirit.

Therefore, no one invoked the right to use this vote of no confidence...at least, in this case.

"Is that all?"

Confident in his victory, the lizard hastened the end of the discussion.

I had no more arguments. In the end, it was a dictatorship ruled by the power of the Guardian Spirits.

But...a familiar voice echoed in the auditorium. This was...unexpected?

"Not yet. Objection!"

Phillip Royals' voice, which had until now not been heard during the debate, became more apparent.

"I will not allow such a student to sully the reputation of Earth!"

"..."

At this declaration, the Guardian Spirit of Earth seemed beyond exhausted.

With his finger pointed at me, Phillip announced his challenge:

"Impostor, face me—with the role of representative at stake!"

The room, which had been completely paralyzed by the Guardian Spirit's presence until just a few seconds prior, began to fill with murmurs.

Inciting pride in one's element, Phillip's simple challenge roused all Earth students to support his cause. This was no surprise coming from the representative candidate; his charisma was exceptionally high compared to someone who had just enrolled in the academy.

Still, something fundamental could not change, so I expressed my disappointment with a sigh. Phillip did not seem pleased by this:

"What's wrong with you?! Are your legs shaking, impostor?"

"If everything could be fixed this way, we wouldn't be having this discussion…"

Visibly enraged by my criticism, Phillip asked why his proposal was invalid. To this, I responded:

"Even if you win this challenge, are you sure you can get the approval of the Guardian Spirit of Earth? He must surely be quite dissatisfied with your performance if his nomination for representative has found its way to me, a first-year!"

It seemed that my words made him lose the dignified attitude he had been keeping; he raised his voice:

"That's just an excuse! If I have to get approval, I'll get it somehow… But you are unworthy of the position!"

He turned his gaze to the Guardian Spirit.

"How is it possible for a guy like him to be appointed as Earth representative? For a first-year student to represent an element that's not his strongest! We demand an explanation!"

I was curious, too, an emotion that was surely shared by all students present.

All eyes focused on that tiny creature that no one would ever believe was one of the legends of the kingdom. He sighed in resignation.

"Do you really want an explanation that you know you will not approve of in the slightest? Do you?"

"Of course we do!"

Phillip's voice met no objections.

Sighing again, the lizard continued, his voice less energetic:

"Simon Anion is fit to be an Earth student, as he is for any other element. In other words…he can be a student of any element."

"How is that possible?!"

"Because he has no element in which he excels."

This shocking response by the Guardian Spirit caused a tomb-like silence. Soon after, a mixture of laughter and irritation followed.

"So that means he is weak? How can he be appointed as representative?"

"'Weak,' you say?"

The voice of the Guardian Spirit became sharp as he silenced the students' rambling.

"His entrance-exam results were hardly brilliant. He passed with the minimum requirement..."

"And what else could that mean if not that he is weak?"

Phillip's question was abruptly interrupted:

"Have I ever called him weak? Do you really think that I would choose a nobody who would easily crumble under the pressure of being my element's academic representative?

"The representative of my element is chosen based not on power but on another standard: a trait that Simon Anion has far more of than any other student."

Curiosity got the better of me, and I entered this discussion for the first time:

"Tell me—what is this trait that I have?"

The Guardian Spirit did not answer.

"Then...how did you realize that such a trait resides within me?"

"Intuition."

"Huh?"

A doubtful air filled the room.

"I told you that you would not like the explanation, did I not?"

The Guardian Spirit had a satisfied expression as if he were mocking all of the students in the room. Phillip lost his temper.

"Then show it to us! Fight me and be crushed like the nobody that you are!"

Phillip's challenge echoed throughout the hall.

Everyone in the audience gazed expectantly at me, but...

"I refuse."

I wasn't the least bit interested.

"You coward!"

Phillip attempted to make a path to reach me, but some students—probably his classmates—held him back.

At that point, a burst of laughter resonated in the hall. It belonged to the Guardian Spirit.

"Interesting... Why not? If Phillip wins, I might even consider appointing him as representative!"

✳✳✳

…And that is how all students ended up gathered in the academy arena.

In the center of a space five times larger than the auditorium to which the students had been summoned for the appointment ceremony, just two students were standing. Everyone else was trying to find a spot in the grandstands.

The arena was the largest of the many training fields accessible to students, as could be seen from the sheer number of spectators it could accommodate. However, even if it could *host* such a large number, this did not mean that it could *seat* them all.

I sighed deeply, my gaze wandering through the crowd of students who hadn't made it in time to get a seat. Standing in the corridor, huddled behind a screen… I wished I could be in their place, not having to worry about the opponent in front of me.

Phillip was drawing a magic circle on the ground, and I was doing the same.

After plowing through the ground instantly with magic, Phillip pulled out a glass vial from the flashy bracelet he wore on his arm and poured the silvery liquid within into a crevasse in the newly drawn magic circle. As he extended his hand toward it, the five rings on his fingers began to glow brightly.

So he wants to compensate in that manner…

I, on the other hand, was carving into the ground with a sword that was small enough to perhaps be better described as a dagger. My worried expression was reflected within the azure hue of the blade.

Although it was possible to cast magic without one, a magical catalyst accumulated and materialized magical power much more efficiently than the human magic circuit could ever accomplish. Catalysts came in many forms, but they were mainly divided into 'material' and 'temporary.'

Material catalysts were specific items that could only be used by the person who owned them. They were synchronized with their owner's magical power through a simple imprinting, but once synchronized with a particular owner, a material catalyst's imprinting could never be changed. As the material-catalyst user's potential grew, the time would eventually come to change catalysts, and this typically caused quite a few problems when trying to recycle the materials.

On the other hand, while everyone could use temporary catalysts, they were consumed on the spot. Their potential was proportional to their user's talent, so it could be said that they were much more powerful than material catalysts.

The reason why we were drawing magic circles was very simple: we had to summon golems to fight in our place. This suggestion was not Phillip's idea, and nor was it the Guardian Spirit's.

It was mine.

I thought back to the moment I accepted the challenge…

***

"Since it was I who was challenged, I have the right to choose the terms of the challenge, correct?"

I received no particular objection to the suggestion that I then gave, but…

"You are not allowed to replenish your golem with magical power."

"What?!"

My condition enraged Phillip.

"Do you know what it is that you are asking me to do? Do you know what it means not to be able to supply your own golem?!"

Naturally, I did. Golems were magical creatures summoned by an individual, and in order to continue existing, they must consume magical power. Without a source, they were destined to disappear.

"You won't even grant a weakling like me this small handicap? Are you perhaps afraid that the weakest will beat the strongest? Although, that wouldn't be a bad show…"

"What are you blabbering about? Advantage or not, I'll beat you all the same! Don't underestimate the legitimate academic representative!"

It's just as I thought…a small provocation is enough to make him lose his reaso—

Before I completed this thought, however…

"So why don't we put a penalty for you? If you happen to lose."

I could only glare in response to this suggestion from the Guardian Spirit.

"After all, I wouldn't want you to lose on purpose, would I?"

He understood exactly what I wanted to do…

✳✳✳

"I'm ready!"

Phillip's voice resounded throughout the arena, bringing me back to the present. The crowd was cheering for him.

The thought that this guy was so popular irked me, but maybe I was the unpopular one… Letting out a tired sigh, I readied myself.

When I finished drawing my magic circle, I bowed with one knee to its center and began to infuse my magical power into it. Since I was not an expert in the magical arts like Phillip, I needed time before I could summon a magical creature as complex as a golem.

I closed my eyes.

From my body to the catalyst, from the catalyst to the ground, from the ground to the furrows, so that the magic circuits…

I felt my body being overwhelmed by magic particles.

…How long has it been?

My control of the magical power became unstable. I bit my lip to calm my thoughts.

I have to stop thinking about it.

There's no need to dwell on the past.

I ran away, and now I'm here to search for a solution.

There's only one thing I have to worry about, and that's all I have to do.

That's why I…

I stabilized the magical output.

I opened my eyes.

I saw my opponent.

In the spotlight, he was waving his hands to the audience.

He's really *underestimating me.*

But I shouldn't worry about his situation. I just had to think about controlling myself.

"I'm ready, too."

Upon my confirmation, Phillip replied with an annoyed tone:

"Took you long enough. I was about to fall asleep!"

"Go right ahead…but don't complain if I wake you up abruptly!"

"We'll see who will be abruptly awakened. I'll prove to everyone that you're not fit to be a representative!"

Phillip was absolutely raring to go.

"I see you are both ready."

The voice of the Guardian Spirit of Earth echoed through the arena.

Letting my gaze wander, I noticed that he was inside a protected platform, together with an elderly man who had a somewhat wrinkled expression. What stood out the most from his figure was his thick white beard and zebra-striped glasses that didn't seem to match his image.

"Then let us not dawdle. Begin!"

The challengers' magical power permeated the field. The spectators' voices invaded the arena. The magical power inside the arena tried to repel these sonic invaders, but since they were shapeless, it could only assimilate them.

Two creatures shaped by magic began to take shape.

Beside each challenger, their presence was perceived by all of the bystanders.

No words were necessary; it was time to fight.

Inside the special platform, I was following the Guardian Spirit of Earth, who had contributed to the fall of the Demon King.

"Domizio, you're a never-ending source of troubles…"

My voice did not hide my fatigue.

"Sorry, Faris, but this year I just can't give up so easily."

The creature's claws were fiercely stabbed into the table he was sitting on.

It wasn't just me who understood his uneasiness very well: most of the professors felt the same way. In recent years, the Earth representatives had been unworthy of their role and done nothing but act for their own benefit. For this reason, I couldn't make a harsh admonishment; however…

My gaze turned toward that first-year student who was positioned atop his magic circle on one knee.

"Why him?"

Whether one looked at his entrance-exam results or his behavior during class, he didn't seem like a particularly powerful or bright student. His theory and practical results were in line with this impression.

However…

Domizio's words interrupted my thinking:

"You know, I followed him to his home."

I sighed again.

"You're really misusing your invisibility spell. And you're also breaching the students' privacy, for that matter. As headmaster, I have no choice but to reprimand you."

In reality, though, I knew that there was nothing I could do about it.

Nobody could restrict Domizio's movements and actions inside the academy grounds, not even me. Still, this childish curiosity was his only solace inside *this artificial prison…*

"So, what impressed you?"

As a *friend*, I couldn't help but get interested too.

"He lives with his sister in an apartment in the academy staff building…but I'm sure you already know that."

"Of course. It was an irregularity, but I couldn't refuse them."

Domizio gave a meaningful mocking smile.

"Oh, you rarely grant that kind of thing."

I knew exactly what he meant. *I* was not the topic of discussion, though.

"Will you tell me what's on your mind, or are you going to keep me in the dark forever?"

Domizio remained silent. I waited a few seconds.

I knew that this silence was meant to tell me that he didn't want to create misunderstandings and wished to express his true opinion.

"His mood was different from what you see on his face now. Tell me, how does it look now?"

I stared at that first-year again. He had reopened his eyes, and within them, an intense light of determination was visible.

"What I saw—was a mask of kindness that covered despair and agony. I saw the eyes of one who wanted to die but couldn't."

I couldn't believe his words.

Watching Simon's expression closely, I couldn't see anything but his iron will, void of any negative tendencies.

"Are we talking about the same person?"

"Are those ugly zebra-striped glasses just for show?"

"I like them, I'll have you know!"

I had a particular complex about the glasses I wore, and even though countless others said they didn't suit me, I continued wearing them anyway. Domizio resumed his speech:

"I wouldn't have believed it either if I hadn't seen it personally. And I don't think even *I* would have noticed if it weren't for one person."

"One person?"

"The reason he can't die. His sister."

I couldn't follow him anymore.

It wasn't that I always could, but I thought I usually understood his line of reasoning… At times like this, however, I received a stark reminder that we were very different beings.

"You mean to tell me that someone so young wants to die already? I would hardly think it possible; he hasn't lived for so long that he would have experienced trauma worth wanting to die over. Or at least…at such a young age, one hardly has a mind mature enough to restrain that impulse."

"That's why I told you that the key to his life is his sister."

I stayed silent.

"I don't know their past, but I am sure of one thing: it is not the length of a person's life that shapes them, but the experiences that they have lived through—a year can pass idly by, while a single experience can cause great upheaval. For this reason, I presume that those two did not have a happy past.

"You should have figured that much out by yourself, right?"

I sighed once more.

"That is correct. I welcomed them because I had a vague feeling that they were in a bad situation, but I did not think they were *that* desperate."

The truth was more complex, but I didn't think it was time to clear it up…or, at least, I didn't want to receive another lecture for ignoring my duties as headmaster. My impression of Simon Anion was that of an extremely mysterious young man, and it seemed like there could be even more to him than I remembered.

It was then that I recalled our first meeting. A shiver ran down my spine, reminding me of that terrible sensation I hadn't felt for a long time…

His gaze of despair.

His gaze of helplessness.

His gaze…of resolve.

Really, who are you…?

While I was reminiscing, the two students finished their preparations. Domizio spoke into the microphone:

"I see you are both ready."

Many gazes turned in our direction, including that of Simon Anion.

No matter how many times I watched him, I saw no traces of the negativity Domizio had talked about. That didn't mean that the reason for which I did not doubt his words was that he was my friend; it was because I knew that he had no reason to deceive me.

Why would a Guardian Spirit bother to lie? To convince an ordinary human being? No—the creature in front of me was far stronger than even me, one of the mages considered the most powerful in the entire kingdom.

"Then let us not dawdle. Begin!"

Loud cheers and a great cluster of magic gathered in the arena.

"Tell me, why did you impose that condition?"

"Hmm… And what might you be talking about?"

He seemed to be playing dumb; I wasn't in the mood to keep him company any longer.

"Let me guess… So that if he loses, he must one day show you his *true* determination?"

With a bored expression, Domizio lazily answered:

"No. Because he has no intention of winning."

005: The Sham

"Then let us not dawdle. Begin!"

After the start signal, the entire arena was shrouded in the students' cheers and the magical power of the two participants. Two male students and a female student wearing a simple blue, diamond-shaped emblem on their chests were watching from a fairly high row of the grandstands. Although they couldn't find a seat, they weren't complaining about practically dangling from the railing; in fact, they were grateful that they were able to set foot in the grandstands at all.

In the center of the arena, a gust suddenly blew, forcing most of the students to shield their eyes from the dust. As the wind weakened, the viewers noticed that the number of silhouettes inside the stage had doubled.

The gust soon calmed down enough to show two figures on one side of the arena. One was a blond student wearing a brown emblem with a lizard inside of it: Phillip Royals. A fully armored knight was kneeling behind him as if swearing allegiance to its lord. But that was no knight; it was the golem he had summoned. This was evident from the fact that its armor, its weapon, and its complexion were all monochrome.

However, many were wondering if it was really a golem.

The knight stood up and positioned itself in front of Phillip, ready to fight. The illusion that they were of the same height was shattered in no time.

A burnished suit of armor holding a sword and shield towered imposingly over its lord. Even if it was an inaccurate estimate, no one believed that this colossus was shorter than four meters.

The accuracy of the detailing and its fluid movements were so smooth that nobody would be surprised if it were a living creature. Its majestic figure and menacing aura were such that no one in their right mind would have any doubts about its strength.

As expected of the strongest Earth student.

None of the bystanders dared to contradict this thought and, although he was disadvantaged by the condition of not being able to replenish his golem's magic, no one even humored the notion that he could lose.

Soon afterward, the wind calmed down on the other side of the arena. There, too, the two silhouettes were around the same height. However, no one would have imagined that…

""""Huh?""""

Mark, Lucas, and Rachael were amazed by the scene. What appeared in front of Simon was…a rather crude golem, to put it lightly. *This* monochromatic figure was nothing compared to the one summoned by Simon's opponent.

With its poorly defined details, one could barely tell where one limb ended and another began. The only part with some semblance of detail was its weapon. It didn't have a shield; it had only a blade that resembled a short sword, identical to the one Simon was holding. This was the creature's only notable feature.

No…there was another one.

"Is that…it?!"

Its height was identical to Simon's while he kneeled inside the magic circle with his catalyst stuck in the ground. Perhaps between fifty and sixty centimeters, the creature immediately became an object of mockery among the entire audience:

"Is he really facing the most powerful Earth student with…*that thing?*"

"Maybe his true calling is the circus!"

"Or he was just bragging a lot."

Lucas and Mark, meanwhile, were expressing their complete and utter surprise:

"He told us he wasn't suited for magic, but I had no idea it was *that* bad…"

"In a way…it's incredible."

"Listen… Do you think Simon did it intentionally to exploit the differences between the golem sizes?"

Rachael had just joined in, asking her brother and his friend for their opinions.

"I don't think so."

A new voice, which they did not recognize, interrupted Rachael.

The three of them turned toward the direction of the voice and saw a female student with a blue emblem and a simple ornament. That chestnut-haired girl was a second-year of Water.

"Even if he was forced by the circumstances, he understood that he couldn't delay things anymore. Since he accepted the challenge, he is surely being serious and simply testing his limits."

The girl talked about Simon in a familiar way, like she knew him. While Lucas and Mark were wondering who she was, Rachael chose to remain silent.

The girl noticed the two students' confusion and smiled at them.

"Excuse me for not introducing myself earlier. My name is Marie Anion, and I'm Simon's older sister."

Lucas and Mark were shocked by her sudden appearance, but Rachael wasn't surprised.

She's his sister. She's obviously going to watch him, no?

"From what I heard, it sounds like you know my brother. Are you in the same class as him?"

Her smile had bewitched Lucas, who didn't hesitate to answer:

"Yes! I'm his best friend, and my name is Lucas Gennari!"

While Rachael and Mark were both thinking, *Since when did you become his best friend?!* Lucas began to introduce them to Marie:

"This is Mark Solus, and he's also a precious friend of Simon's. And this is my sister, Rachael Gennari!"

Both of them wanted to voice an objection, but they stopped when they saw Marie standing still, paralyzed.

"...*Friends*, huh? You finally found friends again, Simon?"

A whisper, or perhaps a murmur—Marie's words were drowned out by the students' cheers, but the three students in front of her heard them as clearly as if she were the only one present. To reassure herself that it was not an auditory illusion, Marie asked for actual confirmation from the people in front of her:

"...You're really Simon's friends?"

Lucas was surprised for a moment by Marie's expression.

"Y-yes!"

Because he was nervous, he stuttered while trying to answer her.

Marie's gaze turned to Mark as if she were asking the same question. Clearly less shaken than Lucas, he answered calmly:

"Yes. Simon is our friend."

Marie nodded as if she were satisfied and turned her eyes to Rachael.

"Are you a friend of Simon's, too?"

Rachael didn't know how to answer. While she was wondering whether she could really consider herself his friend, it was pointless in the end—her brother spoke on her behalf:

"Of course! She's Simon's friend too!"

His passion, which seemed to melt any hesitation, calmed his sister, and she confirmed it:

"Yes. Simon is a friend of mine."

Marie looked at Lucas and Rachael with dreamy eyes, but this lasted only an instant, so the two didn't notice. Mark decided to stay quiet at the sight of something quite familiar.

Suddenly, a clash of swords snapped the four students to attention. They looked toward the center of the arena and saw the two golems engaging in combat. While Phillip's knight was trying to deal a clean hit on Simon's rough statue, the latter avoided all attacks with great agility, causing the knight to do nothing but raise dust.

It was easy to understand why it kept missing; although the area that the knight's sword covered was quite large, it lacked thickness. Since the statue was only a quarter of the height of the knight's sword, it looked like it was riding the winds its opponent generated. Phillip could simply order his knight to use its sword as a fly swatter, but he was too proud to do that, so his knight instead continued relentlessly attacking the statue with correct form.

On the contrary, Simon was still kneeling inside his magic circle. Enveloped in an ethereal glow, he was taking advantage of the match conditions and continuously supplying his summoned creature with magical power. All the while, his golem continued to avoid its opponent's attacks and tried to keep its distance.

"I've got it!"

It seemed like Lucas had just had an epiphany.

"He's trying to exhaust the knight's magical power, then launch his attack and win the match!"

At Lucas's statement, Mark and Rachael sighed.

"W-what's wrong?"

"Didn't you see what Phillip has on his right hand?"

Upon hearing this, Lucas noticed the accessories in question.

"You mean the rings he's wearing? What about them?"

"*Hah...* Why must I have such a stupid brother?"

Rachael gave a sigh, complaining to no one in particular. Mark was about to give Lucas a piece of his mind, but before he could begin, Marie felt obliged to explain the situation:

"The five rings he's wearing are part of one whole catalyst; the one on his middle finger harmonizes with the other four, lessening the strain of using them. This means that he's nudging the barrier of managing five catalysts at once, and on top of this, his golem contains almost twice as much magical power as he usually uses to summon it. This is due to the family treasure he has continued to brag about over the past few years, and it's giving him a considerable advantage."

"Double? With four rings? Shouldn't it quadruple?"

Mark gripped the cross around his neck and prayed, "O Lord, please forgive this fool...," while his sister exclaimed, "How the hell did you pass the entrance exam...?!" with a hand on her forehead, trying to conceal the sight of that useless brother of hers.

Marie smiled. She was amused by the scene and relieved to know that her brother had friends like these.

"Each new catalyst improves the performance of the spell used, but there are diminishing returns, and the spell's efficiency can never exceed twice its original value."

Lucas seemed to understand Marie's explanation, but another doubt came over him:

"Then couldn't we all wear ten rings as catalysts and have the best possible performance?"

"Certainly, if you want to fry your brain."

"Go ahead! Being an only child doesn't sound bad at all…"

"Why are you so mean?!"

Seeing Lucas's eyes begging for forgiveness, Marie deigned to explain the situation:

"It's not so easy to use multiple catalysts. Even a single catalyst weighs heavily on the brain; the limit for a normal person is three at once. Phillip can go one further and use four, which is quite impressive."

"Hmm… Argh, I'm lost here…"

At that point, Rachael, fed up with her brother, greatly dumbed down her explanation:

"Tell me, idiot brother of mine, can you walk and talk at the same time?"

"Hmm? What do you take me for? Of course!"

Shocked by his sister's implication, Lucas's answer was delivered in an irritated tone.

"Then, could you run, sing, read a magazine, review yesterday's lesson, keep an eye on the road for obstacles, and jump over those obstacles all while dribbling a ball?"

"What do you take me for? Of course not!"

"And there's your answer. Doing one thing is simple, while doing several at once is extremely difficult. If you try to use more catalysts than you can handle, you're in serious danger of going into a coma. For reference, a normal student can usually handle only one material catalyst, while professionals can handle two to three. Truly exceptional magicians like the headmaster might manage seven, but no one except the Demon King himself has managed to use eight or more catalysts."

At one point during Rachael's explanation, Marie's expression became somewhat dark, but she did everything she could to return it to normal before jokingly asking:

"Tell me, are you by any chance…everyone's favorite secret informant? Simon has told me about you, but I never imagined you were so pretty!"

Rachael blushed a little.

"They're really siblings…"

Only Mark and Lucas heard her say it, though. As if to change the subject, Mark returned to the main topic:

"Having said that, that knight has a rather high amount of magical energy. To exhaust it completely, it would take maybe forty minutes of intense combat...there's no way this fight will last anywhere near that long, though, with Simon's golem not even attacking."

Since the duel began, the statue had never approached the knight. Perhaps it would be better to say that it couldn't; its every attempt was met with a shield that prevented even the slightest scratch on the knight's armor.

But that didn't mean that every attack had been in vain.

"Ah!"

No one knew which of the three students had let out that cry, but anyone could understand why they were surprised. After countless attacks, Simon's statue was unable to completely evade the opponent's offense. Its left arm was completely detached from its body, falling to the ground and reduced to rubble.

In that same assault, Simon's golem also launched its attack, but...

"!"

One could see a surprised expression on Simon's face. Though his golem's attack had been blocked yet again, this time, it had slightly pierced the knight's shield.

Stepping back, the statue retreated to safety. Taking advantage of that momentary pause, Simon's golem slowly began to regenerate its lost arm...but the opponent knight did not—the small hole in its shield remained.

"How come Phillip isn't repairing his shield?"

Before Rachael and Mark could begin to have another headache...

"Without the complaining ritual, please?"

Lucas's foresight saved him from the usual criticism, making Marie smile. She answered his question once again:

"Normally, that would be the case, but not under the current conditions. Phillip is currently restricted by a limited source of magic. He'll save it for repairing more serious wounds or launching fiercer attacks, not for a bit of damage to a mere shield."

"But if Simon keeps attacking, won't he destroy Phillip's shield sooner or later?"

Marie's expression became slightly darker. An inaudible murmur left her lips... The other three wondered what she had said, but Marie recomposed herself before they could air their doubts.

"Right now, his golem's attacks are too weak to break that shield; the proof is in that hole."

On closer inspection, no other attack by Simon's golem was dealing any actual damage.

"Marie, what did you mean before when you said that Simon was testing his limits?"

Mark and Lucas gave perplexed expressions in response to Rachael's question.

With a giggle, Marie answered without meeting the no-longer-secret informant's gaze, instead staring into the distance at the figure of her brother.

"You know that Simon is quite an unusual mage, right?"

"Yes, but he only told us that he has low magical affinity and is not good at casting spells. But from what I see, besides the height of the summoned golem, he doesn't seem to have any problems."

Lucas was judging Simon to be a reasonable mage. Mark and Rachael thought so, too.

"You know the five variables that are evaluated by the academy, right?"

Lucas's reply was immediate and enthusiastic:

"I know this one! They are materialization, transformation, manipulation, consistency, and sensation."

Marie gave a satisfied smile.

"And can you also tell me why these criteria are evaluated?"

Lucas's face immediately froze, but Rachael threw him a lifeline:

"Materialization is judged on how magic is materialized; that is, created from nothing. This variable is essential for almost all spells, as few are based on existing objects."

"So the golems are an example of materialization?"

Just as Mark and Rachael were about to begin their ritual…

"I get it; I'm wrong, so spare me the lecture!"

Marie again took it upon herself to dispel Lucas's doubts:

"Most Earth magic is based on transforming earth into a suitable form, and golems are no exception."

Lucas didn't completely follow:

"But those golems aren't just a transformation, are they? They're moving, too!"

He pointed to the battle that was taking place in the arena.

"That's because they are also influenced by manipulation, which is how magic can influence matter and move it as the spellcaster wishes."

"And that's not it—"

Following Rachael's explanation, Mark interjected:

"—it's not enough to form a shape and manipulate it; you must also give it a consistency…a physical form that can inflict and absorb attacks, to be able to call it a golem."

Rachael completed Mark's explanation:

"Transformation, manipulation, and consistency are the three main variables on which Earth magic is based, which is why Earth-magic users are usually the least suitable to use magic."

"Huh?"

Lucas's perplexity was clear on his face.

"Isn't using three out of five variables already a big achievement? Why should they be the least suitable to use magic?"

Mark and Rachael sighed deeply.

"Were you not listening? We are discussing the five main variables on which magic is based and why the academy evaluates them."

"All Fire, Water, Wind, and Lightning spells are based on all five of those main variables, plus other minor ones."

At Rachael's and Mark's answers, Lucas was stunned.

"All five of them?!"

Mark, Rachael, and Marie all nodded.

"As for sensation, it's about giving magic real properties. For example, Fire magic is hot, while Lightning magic…zaps. Without this variable, all magic would be pure clusters of magical energy."

Explaining the last remaining variable, Marie went on with the quiz:

"Tell me, what is the standard height of the summoned golem in order to be admitted to the academy?"

"The same height as the summoner."

This time, it was Mark who answered.

"For how many minutes?"

"Huh?"

At Marie's question, all three were left speechless.

"The golem part of the entrance exam is just about two or three minutes, but…"

Mark's answer was hesitatingly interrupted by Marie:

"You know… Normally, my brother can control a golem half his height for up to five minutes. And all it can do is basic movements…"

No one dared to be the first to respond to her revelation.

Five minutes... Half his height... Basic movements... But now...

Their thoughts could easily be read on their faces. At the same time, they noticed Simon's fatigue.

The Water student's visage was covered in sweat and frowning as if he were in great pain. Holding that sword firmly, he continued to maneuver the creature he had summoned, avoiding the knight's onslaught. The knight's shield had deflected all attacks the statue had performed, and this could be seen by the few scratches that barely stained it.

That metal cover, which at the beginning of the battle had been smooth and glittering, now had four or five scratches caused by the four or five somewhat successful assaults of the knight's opponent.

"So does that mean that the longer the fight goes on, the more he's at a disadvantage?"

Instead of answering, Marie gave a mysterious smile.

She said nothing, but the other three knew it was a sign of trust. Just like that, they stopped talking and focused entirely on the fight.

"Damn it…"

I never imagined he would do that*!*

Right now, all I could do was barely avoid Phillip's knight's attacks, thanks to the height difference between the two creatures. Even though Phillip's golem was big, it didn't seem to be influenced by its mass.

This reminded me that magic was an entity that practically defied the laws of physics. It was also established that 'magic' was only the power of the human will to modify what already existed in nature. It was still mysterious and challenging to explain, but although it at times seemed omnipotent, it still had its limitations. For example, no matter how skilled the magician, they would never be able to create ice inside a volcano or transform iron into gold.

You could say that magic was the use of rapid alchemy. What could not exist in nature would remain impossible through magic, and spells required the right conditions to be used. That's why fundamental spells were divided into five main categories, elements that were spread almost everywhere. High-level spells required immensely difficult conditions to manifest, but their effects could be compared to acts of God.

God, huh?

Suddenly, I felt a stabbing pain in my left shoulder.

Looking at the battle, I noticed that I had let my guard down too much: Phillip's knight had taken advantage of my brief distraction to strike my golem's left shoulder, detaching its left arm from the rest of its body.

The audience immediately cheered, as if the battle were already over.

I, too, would've preferred if it were already over, but…

Before it dealt the final blow, I ordered my golem to retreat, and it narrowly escaped total destruction. Gripping my left shoulder to distract me from the pain, I vowed not to lose sight of what was now important.

I don't want to lose.

Even though I had regenerated my golem's arm, I partially reduced its weight so that it could make more nimble movements, and I managed to avoid Phillip's following attacks. His brief jubilation disappeared over time, instead taken over by impatience; he began to prioritize simpler, faster attacks.

It's no wonder.

Since he was limited by my condition of not resupplying his golem with magical power, the longer the fight went on, the more he felt cornered.

But that was also true for me.

Taking advantage of his moment of hesitation, I finally managed to deal some hits, but the attacks were all deflected by the knight's shield. Despite this, that stalwart defense was slowly becoming stained by my golem's assault…although the first attack still left the deepest mark.

I could have continued like this for some time, but I would soon approach my limit. I ordered my golem to retreat, creating a space between the two summoned creatures.

It almost seemed like the calm before the storm.

As I looked around, I noticed something that resembled an egg with emerald green wings. It was a special microphone, protected by a barrier and controlled by the Broadcast Circle that flew around the arena to communicate even the quietest whisper of the participants. I gave it the sign to come closer.

The audience began to intently discuss my intentions. Phillip readied himself for anything.

I raised my hand and showed my index and middle fingers, spread out in a specific manner. Everybody recognized the meaning:

"Two moves."

With these two short words, I captured the attention of all present.

"I'll end this in two moves."

The stunned audience remembered to breathe again and burst into a crescendo of excitement. Although many were excited by my proclamation, the rest were cheering for Phillip.

"How interesting! Go ahead…I'm waiting."

Phillip did not idly stand by.

His knight got into position, accepting my challenge.

Perfect.

It was time to get serious.

Revealing my hand, I increased the power sent to my golem; it now moved far faster than during the previous exchanges. Phillip was surprised, but he adapted quickly. Though it was faster than before, my golem was hardly traveling at a supersonic speed.

At last, the second real clash between the two golems began.

A downward strike by the knight, seemingly sure to hit my golem, was intercepted. The two blades crossed, but it was obvious which one had more power behind it.

But then—the turning point.

Ending the stalemate, my creature slipped its sword under the knight's and proceeded forward. The knight tried to protect itself with its shield…but it would not make it in time.

Using all the strength it had, my golem stabbed its weapon into the armor of the now-defenseless knight…

…but this moment of glory was short-lived. The sword's momentum stopped as suddenly as it had begun. With its weapon stuck, my golem had no way to attack anymore. Having lost the initiative, it was now time for the opponent's counterattack.

Phillip's knight slammed its shield against my golem's face, creating some distance between them. Having suffered a critical blow, I felt a powerful recoil, which made me momentarily lose my concentration.

Taking advantage of the situation, the knight landed another blow. Gritting my teeth, I tried to remain conscious despite all the damage I had just received. My statue rolled a few meters; it was now unarmed—literally.

Only what looked like its chest was still recognizable.

Its 'face,' having had a close encounter with the knight's shield, was marred by a large crack, which reached its abdomen.

It was literally in pieces.

On the contrary, the knight's armor had my golem's sword stuck in its chest but was otherwise practically untouched. It seemed like the winner of this fight was decided. But

—

"Not yet!"

The fight couldn't end—not like this.

Somehow, I managed to get my creature to stand, but it almost immediately collapsed under its own weight, unable to do anything but support itself with one knee on the ground.

Slowly, Phillip's golem approached mine. It seemed as if my summon were kneeling before the victor.

At three steps' distance, the knight raised its sword. Phillip smirked.

"You were right. The match ended with just two moves… Mine."

The knight delivered the coup de grâce.

At least, it should have… However—

Now!

Powerfully kicking off the ground, my golem avoided the death blow and closed in again. Phillip was not alarmed, since my golem had no weapons with which to launch an attack. My golem's charge didn't faze him at all.

At last—there's no need to hold back anymore!

It was time to put my plan into action. I ordered my summon to headbutt the sword that was still stuck in the knight's chest.

It was at that moment that a strange phenomenon occurred, puzzling everyone.

The arena was enveloped in a blinding flash of light, which was immediately followed by an explosion.

***

The wind raised the surrounding dust once more, blocking the view of the two golems. Nobody had expected an explosion at all. There was no doubt that the match was now over, but the outcome was still undecided; Simon's golem was quite clearly in pieces, but just how much damage did Phillip's knight sustain?

The wind stopped blowing, clearing the view of the arena.

Only one golem remained standing, while fragments of the other littered the ground. Phillip's knight was still intact—its armor and shield entirely unscathed.

"Simon's golem was shattered. According to the rules, the winner is Phillip Royals!"

Upon Domizio's announcement, the arena erupted into roars, cheering for the winner.

Simon lay motionless on the ground inside his magic circle. First aid soon arrived, soon deciding to transport him to the infirmary. It was then that the glimmer of the magic circle faded away.

Simon's three classmates were astounded by the final clash, but Marie was absorbed in her thoughts.

What did you mean by the 'What a sham…' *that you gave as you lost consciousness?*

At that moment, no one could answer her question.

- Another point of view -

Strive for perfection.

That was the motto of my family. As I was the only successor to the Fortus family, my parents expected perfection from me, to fulfill the expectations of both the other aristocratic families and the royal family. There wasn't a single moment in my memories that was not filled with rigorous training, whether in etiquette, movement, or magical formulation.

Under this rigid scrutiny from within my own home and from outside it, I was beginning to sense chains closing in on me—not physical chains, but mental ones.

A life full of limitations.

A life full of restrictions.

A life without any choices.

The pressure I endured increased with every day that passed, making me wonder if I was really 'living.' One day, after I turned twelve, I had enough and decided to rebel, talking to my father about it.

"I understand your feelings."

But instead of being relieved from my duties, my father unleashed such great pressure that I could hardly even breathe. Falling to the ground, I barely heard what he was ranting about.

"This isn't it… This is nothing compared to when I was at the academy…"

I honestly thought my father had lost his mind. I woke up on my bed, and my life remained unchanged.

Though I met my father multiple times after that event, I saw no more trace of his madness; it seemed like the discussion I'd had with him had never existed. I never heard his delirious voice again, but his words kept on echoing inside my head.

What happened when he attended the academy…?

The most prestigious magic academy in Gilar was Solset, where the kingdom's elite gathered; there was no doubt that I would soon be sent there as my father was all those years ago.

Just one more year…

I decided to silently endure. I still remembered my father's expression; it was one that didn't hide his jealousy, as if he wanted a chance to be a student again. It wasn't long before I understood what he had meant.

Unaware of anything, I thought it would be an ordinary academy with slightly higher standards than usual. Instead…it was a battlefield. Faced with the power of the Earth representative, I lost everything that I owned: my world view, my dignity, and even my fiancée.

Under the guise of 'giving her special training,' he stole her from me before my very eyes. I began plotting to turn the situation around but soon realized something.

That power… Isn't that precisely what I'm looking for?

The following year, when the academic representatives changed, I saw my supposed fiancée again for the first time since that incident. I could no longer remember what she said, but I was sure it was just a bunch of excuses.

Yet, I forgave her:

"Isn't it normal to be fascinated when faced with such power?"

Lowering myself to the role of a follower of the representative, I saw up close the power that I so craved. The more I observed it, the more confident I became that it was what I had long sought.

I looked forward to my appointment. And when I was so close to getting it…

"The next representative of Earth will be Simon Anion, first-year of Water!"

…another person took what was rightfully mine before my very eyes.

Accepting absurd conditions, I managed to convince him to fight me and came out on top. With the acclamation of all the students, I had proven my worth to everyone. But there was only one person I had to persuade… No, one creature.

Ignoring my opponent on the ground and the unnecessary pleasantries of my followers, I hurried out of the arena and managed to intercept him. I saw that pathetic man who was the headmaster of the academy accompanied by a magical creature who was walking on the wall of the hallway. Approaching them, I made my greetings with the nobles' bow that had been drilled into my body since I was a child.

"Good morning, Mr. Headmaster. And good morning to you too, Guardian Spirit of Earth."

The magical creature didn't even hide his irritation, clicking his tongue.

"I forgot to cast my invisibility spell…"

In a low voice, he was whispering something.

"Good morning, Phillip. Today is such a nice day, don't you think?"

The headmaster was trying to grab my attention against any sense of good etiquette, but I had only one goal:

"Guardian Spirit, as you saw from the duel earlier, I am the most suitable candidate to represent your element."

Surely, he was in a bad mood because his favorite had been defeated by yours truly, but for that very reason, I could not miss this opportunity.

"Please change your mind and give up on that pathetic student!"

"'Pathetic student'? Are you sure it is not *you* who are the pathetic one, fool?"

An incredible wave of pressure slammed into my entire body, making me fall forward.

I broke the fall with my arms. With difficulty, I managed to bring my upper limbs closer to my legs to form a more elegant posture, but I could no longer lift my head.

"I'll only ask this one more time. Who exactly would be this pathetic student?"

Did he notice…?!

I immediately discarded the idea, since I had won as certified by the Guardian Spirit himself. Therefore, I did not hesitate to express my ambition:

"…!"

I was unable to say a thing.

It's the same feeling as back then…!

The atmosphere was tense, until the headmaster's voice broke the stalemate:

"Domizio, we need to talk about that other matter as well…"

After those words, the pressure gradually dissipated.

"You mean that magical creature?"

"We still need to figure out how it got through the barrier, but we already have some suspicions…"

"Humans are such warmongers…"

Losing interest in me completely, the Guardian Spirit decided to continue on his way.

"One small victory, and they think they can win the entire war. They just don't realize —that they are *delusional*."

I was still unable to move. All I could do was listen to their footsteps as they moved further and further away.

It took a few minutes for me to come to my senses. Fortunately, no one saw me in that pitiful state. My hands were shaking. Not from terror…but excitement.

This is the power I've been looking for!

I clenched my fist.

At the moment, I can't even compare to the power of the Guardian Spirit, but if I could just get the title of representative…!

With a rush of adrenaline, goosebumps spread across my back, and I had to wipe drool from my mouth.

I will not allow anyone to take that power away from me…the freedom that I desire!

006: The Aftermath

...Where am I?

I opened my eyes to a place I did not recognize. I was on a bed I didn't know, and white curtains blocked my view.

Just trying to move made my entire body ache. Both my arms and legs seemed completely unusable.

At that moment, I remembered what had happened.

So I lost, huh?

I didn't know how long it had been, but sunlight filtered through the curtains. My best guess was that it was midday or perhaps afternoon, since the battle had taken place in the morning; I was convinced that I'd been unconscious for a few hours.

I heard my stomach rumble. This evidently made my presence known, because someone calmly approached me, dragging part of the curtains away. It was a young man in a lab coat.

He must be in charge of the infirmary.

As if to confirm my thoughts, he introduced himself:

"Pleased to make your acquaintance, Sleeping Beauty. The name's Tonio Frimo, and I'm in charge of this room. I welcome all the wounded, but boys should make every effort not to end up in this ward. Of course, girls are always welcome, wounded or not."

He must truly be an idiot...

I looked at him with pitying eyes, as if he were hopeless.

"Hey, this 'hopeless' guy took care of you for the two days you were knocked out, I'll have you know!"

"Huh?"

I wasn't surprised at the fact that he seemed like he could read my mind, but at the period of time I was unconscious.

"Two...*days?*"

"That's right. For fifty-four hours, you were lying there on that bed. Your sister visited you once, but she didn't seem too worried. Oh, and your classmates came by, too. Are your sister and that girl by any chance interested in becoming my assistants?"

"If you really want assistants, I can introduce you to some. The *male* variety, of course."

The doctor laughed.

"If you have the strength to make jokes like that, you might as well get out of this room."

What kind of treatment is that?

It was at that moment that I shivered. Ignoring the pain that I was feeling, I raised myself forcibly with my back and immediately looked inside the unknown white shirt that I was wearing. Consequently, I realized that there were several magical bandages on my body that stabilized the magic circuit within and, in several areas, ointment was placed to relieve my pain.

But the worst thing was...

Did he see?

Without even giving me time to panic, Tonio turned around.

"I won't ask what happened to your body...but do take better care of yourself from now on."

"..."

I had always known that if I went overboard, I would be unable to move for a while, but I never thought the situation would escalate to this point...

Now what...?

Before I could think of any excuse, a strange noise echoed through the room. Laughing, Tonio dispelled the awkward atmosphere:

"But first of all, I'd say it's better to settle that grumpy stomach, don't you think?"

Holding my hands to my stomach, I tried to stop the grumbling. Tonio took the opportunity to sneak out of the infirmary. Sighing, I swallowed every complaint I had prepared and waited for him.

"It hurts to think on an empty stomach..."

In any case, no matter how hopeless he seemed, his skills were the real deal.

I really did use magic recklessly...

Reflecting on my actions, I came to the conclusion that I should behave and be a good patient.

At the moment, all I can hope is that he doesn't reveal it to others.

At least it's more bearable than...

I flopped onto the bed to avoid thinking about it. The sharp pain and the grumbling of my stomach seemed to be conspiring to make my life hell.

Five, ten, fifteen, and even twenty minutes passed. After thirty minutes, my patience reached its limit:

"What kind of doctor leaves a patient on his own?!"

"The person in charge of this room, I'd say."

An old man with a thick white beard appeared at the infirmary door. From his exquisite red robe adorned with blue embellishments and his composed posture, one could deduce that he was not an average person, but...

"Hmm? What's with that disgusted look?"

"As usual, those zebra-striped glasses clash with your image..."

"Hah, even the youngsters are now lecturing me about fashion! I'll say!"

With implications somewhere between 'I know all too well' and 'But I like them!', his behavior caused his initially noble image to shatter. As if finally remembering the position he held, he coughed once to calm down and introduced himself:

"My name is Faris Crest. I am the headmaster of Solset Academy...although I suspect you already knew that."

I didn't raise an eyebrow.

Having seen him with Domizio, the Guardian Spirit of Earth, in the private room during the fight, I knew that he couldn't have been a simple professor. Besides, it wasn't the first time that I had met him. I wanted to give some words of thanks for everything that he had done for my sister and me, but it didn't seem like the right time.

"Is there a particular reason why you're here, Headmaster?"

Surely, a headmaster wouldn't bother to meet a student just to check on their health... but perhaps the fact that they were a candidate to be an academic representative was quite important in this academy?

"Yes, as a matter of fact."

His tone became more severe. I had a bad feeling about this...

"I must inform you that you have been transferred from Water to Earth."

...which had just come true, albeit not the worst scenario that I had envisioned.

"Does it by any chance have anything to do with my being a candidate to represent Earth?"

Compared to receiving the news that I had been appointed as a representative without my consent, the fact that I'd merely been transferred was...less troublesome.

Not by much, though.

Sighing, the headmaster nodded. I sighed too and tried to ask something, fighting the feeling that it would be meaningless:

"And naturally, I cannot refuse, correct?"

"Don't ask questions you already know the answer to."

"It never hurts to try."

If Domizio had already rejected my refusal to become his representative, it was quite obvious that he would be rather strict with this transfer as well.

"There are no circumstances under which I could stay in Water?"

I was hoping for a miracle from the headmaster... What I actually got was far from that, though:

"You could make the Guardian Spirit of Earth lose interest in you? I'd say that would be the only possibility."

I sighed again.

It's hopeless.

"I don't even know why he set his eyes on me..."

It's not because of what I did at the start of the year...right?

Denying that possibility, the headmaster seemed not to share my opinion:

"I might just have discovered why."

Concerned, I carefully listened on.

"Individuals like you are rare, after all. Your problems lie not with the five main variables of magic—but *with fundamental magic control itself.*"

I sighed, and the headmaster took that as a sign that he had the right idea.

I didn't get discovered.

The fact that he understood the kind of issue I had with magic was actually incredible, but it didn't bother me much. After a battle like that, it was only natural that someone like him would notice.

"As the name implies, fundamental magical control is essential to cast a spell, and it is not a basic factor but a fundamental requirement for any spellcaster."

I nodded in agreement.

"This requirement distinguishes people who can use magic from those who cannot...or exposes the fact that their magical capacity is so incredible that they are unable to control it."

He was not wrong; I was a being of extraordinary magical capacity that an average person could not hope to control.

But that was not the whole truth about me. Tightly gripping the bedsheet, I couldn't help but remember *that* moment. The headmaster kept talking:

"The explosion at the end of the fight was caused by you no longer being able to control yourself and the spell going berserk, was it not?"

Magic that has gone out of control was considered 'berserk.' Without fail, it would end up self-destructing, causing an explosion that would affect everyone—whether an ally, an enemy, or a bystander—within range, irrespective of the purpose of the spell. Even defensive magic that went berserk could harm instead of protect.

I remained silent, choosing not to correct him.

"I'd be very curious to see what you could do if you had more mastery over your magic, and I believe the Guardian Spirit of Earth is of the same opinion."

I smiled mockingly.

"Is something the matter?"

"No, it's nothing."

I was reflecting on my duel with Phillip and its conclusion.

"Could you relay a message to the Guardian Spirit for me?"

"Hmm? What is it?"

"Let's see... How about: 'I'll make no fuss about the transfer, but don't even dream that I'll follow the arrangements, since you didn't respect them first.'"

Although he could not possibly understand the meaning of my sentence, the headmaster accepted my message without any questions.

"I truly hope you can save Earth..."

Now it was my time to be puzzled.

"What do you mean by that?"

He refused to answer, only giving me a mysterious smile.

"I'm sure you'll learn this soon enough, from a fairly neutral source."

Before I could even reply, he ended the discussion:

"After all, hearing it from one of the parties involved isn't very convincing, is it?"

For a second, I didn't know how to answer.

He seemed to have fairly high expectations. But that didn't concern me.

"As I said before, I have no intention of becoming an academic representative."

Having said my piece, I struggled to stand up. I took my clothes, which were folded neatly on a nearby chair, and tried to leave the room.

"Oh, right..."

Remembering one thing, I turned to the headmaster, who watched me seemingly with no intention of telling me to stop and rest awhile.

"And tell him to stop using invisibility, infiltrating other people's homes, and eavesdropping."

Before the headmaster's surprised gaze, I opened the infirmary door.

"Next time, I'll grab him by the tail…"

I closed the door, distancing myself from the room.

When I felt that I was alone, I collapsed, supporting myself on the wall. Even though I had put on a brave front, my body was screaming in pain.

"'Save Earth,' huh…"

Even though I had suddenly been transferred, I…no, I didn't have to think about it; it wouldn't do me any good to worry.

I just had to prepare for the worst, in anticipation of what tomorrow might bring.

007: The Beginning II

"And so, from today onward, Simon Anion will be joining our class."

After completing his speech, my new professor gave me some time to introduce myself. Unlike my first day at the academy, however, I was greeted with looks full of suspicion and disdain by my classmates, making me deeply uncomfortable. The only silver lining was that Phillip and I were in different years, so it was impossible for us to be in the same class.

"...I'm Simon Anion, and I've just moved into your class from Water. I hope we'll get along."

After my brief introduction, I walked to the only empty desk in the class, which was in the back row. My classmates' stares seemed unceasing and continued even after I sat down. I pretended to ignore them and looked under my desk for my textbooks, as I had done on my first day in Water.

What I discovered there, however, was not an ordinary set of textbooks. Every sheet of paper was covered in ink—words whose contents were all too easy to figure out. As soon as the other students saw what I had noticed, laughter began to fill the classroom.

I sensed feelings of spite and resentment toward me. I closed my eyes and took a deep breath, then another. I opened my eyes—and sneered. Those who saw my smile stopped laughing immediately.

If that's what they want, then so be it!

"Professor, my textbooks are all smeared!"

Playing the part of an astonished student, I loudly explained my situation.

"What?"

The professor approached my desk and found my textbooks, all practically illegible. He sighed, before saying something that completely stunned me:

"There's nothing we can do about it. For the time being, make do with them."

"...Huh?"

Not believing my ears, I saw the professor return to his desk and begin the lesson. After giving me a mocking smile, the other students turned around and listened to the lecture. All I could do was sit down and struggle through those unreadable books, trying to gather what little meaning I could from the few words that could still be seen. Throughout the lesson, I heard the incessant snickering of what should be my class*mates*. I could only bite my lips, trying to contain my emotions.

When the intermission bell finally rang, it was the first time I had felt so relieved by a break in quite some time. I rested the side of my head on my desk, trying to relieve all the stress I had accumulated, but not even five seconds of comfort later, I saw some students approaching me. There were five in total, and the student in front seemed to act as their representative.

"Nice to meet you. I am the class monitor; if you need anything, you can ask me."

Relieved by an unexpected oasis in this desert of malice, I tried to take advantage of the opportunity that had presented itself before me:

"Perfect timing—I was wondering where I could change these textbooks…"

"Oh?"

With that one word, the atmosphere became tense. His gentle tone morphed into something far more malicious.

"Did the professor not say that there was nothing that could be done and that you had to make do?"

I already knew very well how this would end, but I still didn't want to give up my only hope of establishing a good relationship with my new class.

"But I can't take classes under these conditions, so I was wonder—"

"Mm… Maybe there is a solution, after all…"

Hearing his words, I had the illusion of a happy ending.

"…but how about you go get me a drink first?"

"…Huh?

"All this talking has made me *quite* thirsty. You would do well to get me a *little* something to drink; isn't that right?"

He turned his head to a nearby student.

"Oh, yes. Actually, now that I think about it, I'm also a bit thirsty."

"While you're at it, do get one for me as well."

Soon, almost all of the students had told me what to pick for them.

"Come on. Wouldn't it be bad if you disappointed the expectations of all your classmates?"

"…"

I was a fool to hope that I could fit in.

"…Hey…"

One of the five raised his voice.

"…Don't you think you're taking this a bit too far? That's no way to treat a classmate."

Perhaps he was the oasis that I was looking for.

"What?!"

The class monitor turned around to look the lone dissenter in the eye—a typical student with dazzling straw-colored hair. Although the neck warmer he wore was conspicuous, what was truly eye-catching was the two material catalysts he carried on his belt. Judging by how he wore his pair of tonfa—Eastern weapons similar to batons—around his waist, I wouldn't have been surprised if he were part of the disciplinary committee.

"I'm not mistreating him; I just asked him for a favor. The whole class is my witness, right?"

"That's right."

"We all heard it."

"Get us a drink, already!"

Soon, he found himself cornered.

I sighed deeply. This was undoubtedly the oasis that I was looking for, but I couldn't go near it. If I got any closer, the oasis would disappear.

It was a mirage.

I gathered all of my textbooks and tried to leave the class, but the class monitor blocked my way out.

"Oops… I haven't told you what I want to drink yet, right?"

"…Get out of the way."

Shaking his head as if he had judged me to be hopeless, he stepped aside, but just as I tried to exit the room, he grabbed me by the shoulder.

"This element does not welcome to you. Go back to where you came from and let Phillip become the academic representative—you have no place here."

I gritted my teeth, shrugged my shoulders to get him off me, and made my leave, successfully this time.

"He's got a lot of nerve…"

"To duel Phillip on such advantageous terms and lose on top of that…"

"You can clearly see that the Guardian Spirit is favoring him."

"I would never trust a guy like that!"

Even though I had left the class, I could still hear the voices of my classmates very clearly. Their dissatisfaction was clearly rooted very deeply.

With quick steps, I got as far away from that place as possible. A student tried to chase me, but he stopped as soon as he left the room with a pant and a sigh; my figure was no longer visible.

***

Once I had reached a corridor where I couldn't see or hear anyone else, I stopped and sat with my back against the wall. I stared upward, tired.

"…You saw how it turned out, didn't you?"

A passing observer might have thought that I was talking to the wind… I was not.

"You had to realize that it would end like this. This is torture for me."

There was still no answer. Even though I had my eyes closed, I put an arm in front of my face as if shielding it from the sun and said the magic word:

"Don't you think you owe me at least *one* answer, Domizio?"

In that instant, a faint glow illuminated the corridor, and a brown lizard the size of an iguana appeared on the wall I was leaning against.

"…When did you notice?"

"It would be strange if you *weren't* watching me."

After all, I'm the reason you're causing so much trouble in the academy.

I sighed, resigned myself to gravity, and lowered my arm.

I opened my eyes but did not look at Domizio. I could hear the voices of students having fun outside the open windows that were circulating the seasonally appropriate cold air, and my current situation made me feel an indescribable jealousy.

"…"

"Why so silent?"

"Because I care about my tail."

It took a few seconds before I understood Domizio's response. When I finally figured it out, I began to laugh uncontrollably.

"So the headmaster really did relay my message, huh…"

"Why wouldn't he?"

From his innocent tone, it seemed that the Guardian Spirit didn't understand the true meaning of my message and was merely treating it as a simple warning. Perhaps I was underestimating the headmaster's power or the connection that the two of them had?

A mere student was threatening a Guardian Spirit… No one in their right mind would consider the notion anything other than a bad joke, yet I had done it for real, and Domizio's acknowledgment of my threat seemed to laugh in the face of common sense.

And there was only one reason why I had made that threat:

"Everyone would be on their guard after noticing that their home had an uninvited guest, no? Especially an *invisible* one."

"…People usually don't find me if I'm invisible…"

"*That's* your excuse?"

"I beg for your forgiveness."

Sensing the barely hidden anger in my voice, Domizio admitted his fault and sincerely apologized. The Guardian Spirit was behaving completely differently from the last time I had encountered him. All the pressure and presence that he had previously displayed vanished. To show this weakness in front of me…

"What is the issue within Earth?"

Approaching that topic, I finally looked at him, before continuing:

"The problem is certainly not with the pride that they feel for their element; rather, this is a good thing. Boasting about something, or even about yourself, rarely leads to serious issues. One can become arrogant, but that doesn't seem to me to be the main problem."

However, to my surprise, Domizio remained silent.

"You won't tell me anything…because you're biased?"

I took his continued silence as affirming my suspicions. It seemed that I should take another route to uncover what was happening inside the element.

Will I forever be unable to choose my destiny…?

My thoughts were interrupted by the ringing of the academy bell. I unwillingly got up.

"It's time to head back to class…"

Before I set out, I asked a question to the Guardian Spirit of my new element, even though I knew that it was stupid:

"I can't skip class, can I…?"

The silhouette of that brown lizard, which should normally have made an imposing figure, seemed to shrink. This time, I took his silence as denial. I turned my back on him, and just when I was about to leave…

"…The only thing I can do is change those textbooks."

I heard his voice in the distance as he disappeared from sight.

"Go to the professors' lounge after class. I'll make them change the books for you."

I sighed at his words.

"That's not much from a Guardian Spirit…"

As if I had hit a weak spot, the atmosphere became quite unpleasant. Even before I took a step, Domizio asked me one last question:

"…What are you going to do about the lessons?"

This time, it was my turn to be silent.

Although this series of events was within my predictions and I had a proper countermeasure ready, I couldn't bring myself to say it. After a few seconds, the words came out of my mouth very hoarsely:

"Only one thing…ignore them."

Without waiting for a response, I set off to my new academic life.

- Another point of view -

"Only one thing…ignore them."

After he gave that response, the boy's eyes lost the dim light that had illuminated them, and his gaze became gloomy enough to make me feel shivers down my spine. Unable to stop him, I could only watch as his lonely back shrank into the distance.

What was *that?*

When he spoke those words, I felt a strange negative force…as if gravity had multiplied out of nowhere. That pressure…made me remember *that moment*. Scenes from the past flashed in front of me, and I shook my head to dispel them.

The past cannot be changed.

I was able to shrug most of the memories—except one.

It was a cold, rainy day.

The day I cursed my lack of power.

The day I lost my only partner.

The day I lost a part of myself.

The dull sound of a book falling in the distance brought me back to the present, and that memory faded once more into the deepest recesses of my mind.

Right now, I had other worries; I had no time for confusing the past with the present. *He* was no longer here.

And no one knows this better than I.

I hurried to infiltrate Simon's class as if trying to divert those thoughts from my head, and it worked all too well.

What the…?

I sensed a tense atmosphere even from outside the classroom. If the morning was filled with the students' malicious laughter, the present was filled with nothing but the professor's trembling voice. And the cause of it…was Simon.

He wasn't doing anything special. He was flipping through the pages of the vandalized book and taking notes, which he then proceeded to write down in a separate notebook. His concentration was truly intimidating—one of his hands was flipping through the book, and with the other, he was transcribing.

I doubted he was even listening to the professor.

When a student on the side tried to distract him, Simon glared at them, causing them to back off with a jump and making a ruckus in the process. Simon soon lost interest and returned to his scribbling.

The atmosphere remained heavy until well past the end of the lesson; even the lunch break did not help ease the tension. While Simon continued his transcribing, all of the others fled from the class, only to return reluctantly at the ringing of the bell—not even the start of the next lesson eased the intimidating aura that surrounded Simon.

No one even dared go near him.

So that's what you meant by 'ignore them'?

It seemed more like a threat. Everyone, professors included, was carefully watching the hands of the clock placed at the side of the classroom, waiting for the end of this hell. When the bell rang, still no one dared move; they were all watching the actions of that diligent student.

Simon was picking up his books and preparing to leave when a student stood in his path, attempting to stop him. His response?

"…Move aside."

"Hey, don't you think you're a bit full of…"

"I said, *move aside*."

When Simon repeated himself, the class monitor jumped unconsciously. His tight grip on Simon's shoulder weakened, and his hand retreated on its own. The class monitor's face panicked, and he stepped aside as if by instinct.

Simon left the classroom.

"What just…?"

The class monitor's murmur was followed by more from the other students, but I did not care enough to know what they were talking about.

I followed Simon and saw that he went to the professors' lounge. After explaining his situation, he found resistance from some professors. It seemed that I had underestimated Phillip's charisma: it was evidently more deeply rooted than I had imagined. Just as I was about to intervene, Faris appeared and approved Simon's request. His appointment as headmaster of the academy had been recognized by the kingdom itself, and no one dared contradict him.

After having his books replaced, Simon left the room immediately. I decided to postpone any pleasantries with Faris to pursue this troublesome student.

He did not head toward the exit but instead entered the library. Inside this lighter atmosphere, he continued to scribble away at his notebook and revise his previous notes without ever stopping.

Still, no one dared approach him.

His eyes, devoid of light, never turned away from his new textbooks and the notebook he was using. This seemingly never-ending process was repeated throughout the afternoon until the sun began to set.

He gathered his belongings and left the library. I immediately heard a sigh of relief from everyone inside it. I ignored those poor bystanders; Simon was finally returning home.

As he walked through the evening forest, his path was lit by decorated lamps, powered by us Guardian Spirits. Also functioning as a repellent against magical creatures, the lamps would keep all who passed through the ground that they illuminated safe and sound.

Walking up the stairs of the staff building, I tailed Simon silently. It wasn't that I had forgotten his warning. My tail was in danger, but I felt responsible for his current situation. I made up my mind and continued to chase him.

I had no idea how he did it, but it seemed like he might already have realized that I was following him. However, he said nothing and went on as usual.

In front of his apartment door, he took out his house key and sighed deeply. Quite exhausted, he gave an 'I'm home' as he opened the door. The answer that he received in return, however, was far from tired:

"Welcome home!"

A girl with a chestnut ponytail beamed at him affectionately. Wearing a kitchen apron with weird green spots, she extended her hands toward Simon.

As if Simon had just noticed something obvious, he walked toward her and fell into her arms. His sister's expression became even softer, while his own slowly regained color.

I could no longer feel any trace of the pressure that had been oozing from him ever since that discussion we had held. Slowly, his face softened and he gave an unexpected smile. With a few tears in his eye, he responded to his sister:

"Thank you."

I was relieved. Even though those words weren't meant for me, knowing that he had a figure he could rely on made me feel so much better as I watched from outside the apartment door.

I guess it's time to go.

I was about to leave when I decided to do something stupid: I closed the door. He would definitely be able to tell that I had been watching him, but it was the least I could do to repay him.

Your time with your sister, at least, must be private.

Thinking back to his expression after he had been pampered by his sister, I couldn't help but overlap his figure with the only human I had ever had close ties with. He, too, had truly cared about his bond with his sister…

And when that bond broke, that man had lost his mind.

Kinlarus, the Demon King—that was what that man was later named.

***

"Hmm…?"

Seeing my sister's puzzled face, I couldn't help but wonder what was on her mind.

"Ah… Simon, the door closed itself…"

Convinced that it was the work of that Guardian Spirit, I could only sigh.

"Don't let it bother you."

Reassured by my words, Marie nodded and lost interest in the mystery of the self-propelled door. With one hand, she fixed my hair as usual. It tickled a little, but I said nothing. As soon as I regained some composure, I left my sister's arms.

"I'm better now."

"You could always let me spoil you some more."

Even though her tone was mischievous, she left me without any complaints and returned to the kitchen. Hearing the sounds of water being boiled and vegetables being diced, I felt at ease.

Yesterday, Marie had insisted that she would take care of tonight's dinner before forbidding me from coming home early. She'd told me that she was worried I would start cooking without telling her, but I know that that was just an excuse. Surrendering to her request, I had spent the afternoon getting ahead with my studies.

"Haaah…"

Heaving a long sigh, I sat in a chair at the table set for two, holding one of the many books that were displayed on a wall-mounted bookcase that took up most of the short side of the room. I could have sat on the couch that was next to the bookcase, but I decided to position myself at a shorter distance from my sister.

"What happened today?"

With her back facing me, Marie asked her question without any expectations.

"Nothing special... I was just thinking about how I won't be able to use the library anymore."

"Were you absorbed in books again? I feel sorry for the students who were in the library with you."

Slightly hurt by her comment, I couldn't argue. I heard her giggle merrily.

"Simon... You should get a grip on yourself when you're studying, you know? You're not racing to find an answer anymore, right?"

Clutching the book in my hand, I barely had the strength to answer, but I was able to give voice to a weak 'You're right.'

As if interrupting me, my sister cheerfully brought our dinner to the table.

"Come on, let's eat!"

Among the various vegetable dishes, what stood out the most was a hot soup with fish and tomato sauce. Seeing what was for dinner, I couldn't help but let out another long sigh.

"Listen, Marie..."

"Yes, what is it?"

My sister's expression was satisfied, since she had been able to prepare so many dishes at once, but...

"...one day, I'll have to teach you how to cook..."

Except for the soup, the rest of the dishes were only washed and lightly seasoned vegetables.

"But I prepared the soup!"

"...With the fish I cut yesterday and the tomato sauce I stored the day before?"

My sister's figure was shrinking.

"But... But... I put it all in the pot and heated it!"

She seemed like she was searching for any reason to be praised, but I didn't fight back, instead giving in. Under pressure, I fed myself a spoonful of soup.

"...It's good."

Unexpected praise left my mouth; it certainly tasted richer than the usual dishes my sister prepared. She patted my head, seemingly happy with my compliment.

"Thank you."

With an expression that I knew all too well, Marie looked me in the eyes. I looked away and focused on dinner.

That's not good.

I tried to conceal the embarrassment by scarfing down everything on my plate, but it was inevitable that, sooner or later, something would go down the wrong pipe. I drank the glass of water that my sister promptly poured for me, and it took a few seconds before I could finally swallow the piece of vegetable stuck in my throat.

I didn't know whether she or I started, but we began laughing heartily. No heavy atmosphere was in sight around the house.

My sister's smiling face is all I need.

Since my sister had prepared dinner, I forcibly took the duty to clean the dishes, and Marie surrendered. From the utensils used and the almost full trash can, I was able to confirm my suspicions about why she had driven me away from home.

Clearly able to see just how much my sister had pulled out all the stops to prepare dinner, I responded by rolling up my sleeves and commencing work with 120 percent effort, not giving any words of reproach about how much waste she had created. Starting with the dishes, I soon moved on to the pots and pans.

Meanwhile, my sister was sitting in the chair that I had used during dinner, and, looking at the book that I had taken from the bookshelf, she removed her hairband.

"...*The Venom of Snakes*, huh...?"

When I heard the title of the book that I had been reading, my hands froze for a moment.

"Simon... You know that you no longer..."

But Marie did not continue. I gave a sigh in response.

"I have no more interest in that matter, but reading has become the only thing that can make me relaxed."

I omitted the obvious 'besides being next to you,' but my sister's expression did not lighten. Instead, she bit her lips and tried to change the subject.

"Listen... How's your new class?"

This time, it was my turn to bite my lips. I knew that if I told her the truth, it would worry her as it had in the past.

However...

I sighed once more and told her the truth.

"It's hard for me to—no, I don't think I'll fit in at all."

My hands, which had just stopped, started cleaning the pots once more. Noticing my gloomy expression, my sister asked me another question:

"Didn't your friends come to see you?"

Puzzled, all I could do was tilt my head to one side.

"Friends?"

"Mark Solus, and Lucas and Rachael Gennari."

When I heard those names, I couldn't help but be surprised.

"…When did you meet them?"

"Three days ago, when you dueled Phillip."

They were there too, huh?

"Maybe they were busy with the Water classes and…wait a second."

Marie couldn't help but wonder what had happened, since I rarely reacted like that.

"I just remembered that they visited me in the infirmary and I haven't thanked them yet. I wonder if they already know I've woken up…"

Marie laughed cheerfully.

"You shouldn't underestimate any aspect of everyone's favorite secret informant—especially not her beauty! I wish my class had an informant this cute too!"

Refraining from the punchline of 'So secret informants are a normal thing?', I simply humored my sister and gave a slight chuckle.

"I'll have to thank them properly."

Without any hesitation, Marie presented her plan:

"So how about I call them for you? That shouldn't be a problem, right?"

Her eyes shone with excitement.

"In that case, you take care of it. That said, you were already planning to contact them, weren't you?"

She playfully gave herself a light tap on the head and stuck out her tongue.

"You got me!"

I couldn't help but sigh, but I soon smiled instead.

"Where shall we meet? Here?"

Evidently, however, Marie already had a place in mind:

"You know that little room with a constantly rotating globe on the fourth floor?"

Comparing the general layout of the academy to what I had observed from visiting the building in person, I tried to find the room my sister was talking about.

"Yes, I know the one. But isn't it always closed?"

Marie smiled mysteriously.

"Then you don't need me to show you the way. We're lucky there's such a convenient landmark in the room!"

"I guess I have the tour guide to thank for knowing where to direct my sight."

Not my physical sight, but my *magical* sight.

Although it was a part of my powers that I would have preferred to keep sealed forever, its ability to facilitate analysis of my surrounding environment was far too useful for me to keep it locked up *permanently*. Usually, it was a very useful technique, but…

"Had I known that the Guardian Spirits look like animals, I would have ignored them or not used this power at all…"

Marie laughed merrily.

"Well, what's done is done. It's no use crying over spilled milk!"

She could certainly say that, but that was probably the cause of my downfall. Sighing deeply, I tried to ignore the matter; there was nothing I could do about it now.

"So, what caught your curiosity?"

With that question, my sister reconfirmed the fact that she knew me all too well; although these eyes of mine were very helpful, I did not use them every time.

Despite having lived within the academy grounds for nearly six months, it was only recently that I first entered a building connected to the academy's study program. This wasn't something to be surprised about, since I was already quite busy training in the morning, studying in the afternoon, and working part-time in the evening while also having chores to do in my spare time.

And yet…

"…When I set foot in the building, I had a strange hunch."

Hearing my words, Marie became tense. This was the first time during my stay at the academy that I had felt such discomfort; it was as if a strange magical power permeated the building.

After confirming my feeling, I also checked the other academic buildings and realized that most of them were in the same state. Wrapped in a thick magical mantle, as if it were protecting them, but at the same time…

"'When a mage has a hunch, they must not ignore it'…right?"

My sister's voice made me stop thinking pointless thoughts any further. Biting my lips at that quote, I knew that my sister was doing the same. No matter how much I didn't want to admit it, *his* words had always been correct.

As if to dispel the tension, my sister asked me to continue. I took a deep breath, before resuming my explanation:

"At first, I thought there was something dangerous hidden in one of the rooms of the academy *buildings*, but I was wrong."

For official purposes, the entire academy was accessible to all students, but in reality, it was divided into five areas, each belonging to one of the five elements. The territories outside the buildings were mainly referred to as practice or combat zones, but some places were for the exclusive use of a particular element or person. For example, only their respective members could access each element's dormitory common room or the student council room without a specific reason. Other such cases included the academic representatives' private lounge and the ceremony hall.

Nevertheless, accompanied by the right person, any student could access any place in the academy…provided that they were strong enough to protect themselves and their companions in case of emergency from the dangers that they would face within. Such 'emergencies' happened quite frequently, since the academy did not provide its own materials for personal experiments and forced students of different elements to collaborate as though facing a real adventure.

My sister had told me that all of the academy *grounds* were accessible…

"…However, what about *below* the academy?"

008: The Oasis in the Desert

The sound of the academy bell announced the start of the lunch break. I quickly gathered my things and quite literally ran away from the classroom, despite it being my classmates who were the terrified ones. They were much more relaxed today than they had been yesterday, but that didn't mean that the pressure I was unleashing half unintentionally and half on purpose could easily be withstood…they did deserve it, though.

At the sight of my escape, both the students and the professor gave a collective sigh of relief. I couldn't see the class monitor, and obviously, I didn't want to see him, either. In any case, he probably wouldn't end his harassment just because of some threats.

If they had stopped after so little, I wouldn't have suffered so…

I quickly shook my head and tried to forget about it. I shouldn't let myself be restrained by the past. I promised myself that this time I would not let my sister worry about me for stupid reasons like this.

I quickly climbed the stairs and came across the room that my sister had told me about. It had a door that was practically identical to all of the others, with the sole difference being that it was the only one without a plaque explaining the room's function. I stared at the key in my hands and recalled yesterday's discussion.

***

"It used to be the Astronomy Club, but it was closed for various reasons, and I obtained the right to use the room to study with my friends."

Upon hearing those words, I hesitated for a moment:

"That doesn't mean…"

"It's all right—"

In a slightly louder voice, my sister interrupted me.

"—I've been using it for a year, and that's all I need. Now I want *you* to use it."

"But…"

"I'll tell my friends and we'll make arrangements. It wouldn't hurt to study in our rooms once in a while."

I could no longer argue. It was the room in which she had strengthened her friendships for a year and finally found a glimpse of happiness.

"Don't worry about me; start using that room for yourself."

Marie was smiling. Though I had wanted to protest, I knew that I could no longer object in front of that smile.

"For myself, huh…"

***

Those words had no meaning to me. Yet, my sister always tried to do what was best for me.

Even though I…

"Hello there!"

I heard a dull sound—almost like a pat on the back… No, it *was* a pat on my back. I turned around and saw three students the same age as me: Mark Solus, and Lucas and Rachael Gennari. By the way, the one who had patted me was Lucas, and he was…being strangled by Rachael, all while Mark watched on without batting an eye.

I couldn't help but smile at this peaceful situation. When Lucas's face began to turn blue, I decided to help him.

"Rachael, I think that's enough."

At my words, Rachael freed her brother, who was now idolizing me as his savior.

"Have you been waiting for a long time?"

Mark answered simply:

"We've just arrived. We saw you at the door, but you weren't moving, so this guy decided to come forward."

"Who are you calling 'this guy,' huh?"

"*This* guy."

Mark jabbed his finger at Lucas, and the two of them started tussling. Rachael sneaked up on me.

"Are you okay? You had a dark look on your face."

Facing her honest concern, which was most likely shared by the other two, I could not help but smile.

"Don't worry. I'm much better now."

I raised my voice and called out to the other two:

"Hey, we're locking you out!"

In response to my call, they stopped fighting and followed us into the room.

In front of me, in the center of the room, there was a rather large rectangular table with five chairs surrounding it. On either side of the room, four shelves full of books covered the walls, leaving no space for any decorations other than a globe that depicted not the kingdom and surrounds but the sky. Powered automatically, it seemed to follow the movement of the stars, making it an indispensable object for any astronomy fanatic.

Opposite from the door, there was a rather large window that covered half the wall, and another door leading to the balcony. From what I saw, there were few rooms with balconies; this must be why the former Astronomy Club had occupied this room. Although I was curious about the books around me, I resisted the temptation and sat down on one of the five chairs available. Rachael sat in front of me, Lucas sat next to me, and Mark sat next to Rachael.

I addressed everyone:

"Please forgive me for not informing you when I woke up."

Forget minding my words; Lucas was smiling.

"Don't worry. Rachael told us right away when she heard you'd recovered, and we knew you had a lot on your plate."

Looking at Rachael, I could only apologize.

"Sorry for the trouble. I should have at least let *you* know, since you're the informant."

"No problem. I enjoy collecting information, after all."

Her statement reminded me of yesterday's discussion. I wanted to tell her the nickname my sister and I had come up with, but considering how hard I was having to suppress my laughter, perhaps I shouldn't, after all.

"Hey, what's going on?"

Rachael was clearly upset, although she didn't know why.

"I'm sorry; I was just remembering something amusing about my sister…"

Finding the right moment, Mark entered the conversation:

"Speaking of your sister, I never thought I'd see her coming into our class."

"She was really worried about you, you know? Don't ever do that again!"

"Look who's talking…"

Hearing Lucas and Rachael bicker like this, I gave a small smile.

"So, what did she say to you?"

"Ah, well…"

Rachael hesitated slightly, refusing to meet my eyes. Mark interjected:

"She was wondering if we were free, then requested us to come to this room to see her dear brother and continue to be friends with him."

"And then she kept flattering my sister, only to then embarrass her with a ridiculous nickname. Isn't that right, 'Informant Too Pretty to Be Monopolized by One Class'?"

Between Mark's response and Lucas's teasing laughter, Rachael was seriously considering flinging the free chair in fury. However, since it was at the opposite end of the table, she gave up on the idea, instead launching a verbal offensive:

"Says the loser who blushed while talking with Marie?"

After his sin was exposed, Lucas began waving his hands wildly through the air. He ended up pleading to me:

"I-it's not what you think! Your sister is so pretty that I couldn't help it! Gosh, what did I say?! Please don't kill me!"

Seeing him panicking, I couldn't help but laugh.

"That is correct; my sister is indeed so pretty that one can't help but blush when one's eyes make contact…but isn't it the same for your sister, too?"

"U-um…"

Charmed by my sweet talk, Rachael started wildly waving her hands as well. Mark and I couldn't help but laugh at the flustered siblings and comment:

"You really say some embarrassing things…"

"One should never underestimate the power of he who loves his sister."

And that's the story of how I made my first real bond in this place.

"U-um… Aren't you hungry?"

Midway through trying to pull herself together, Rachael put her lunch box on the table; so did Mark and Lucas.

"Hmm? Don't you have your own lunch, Simon?"

When Lucas asked that question, the other two's eyes focused on me.

"Don't worry about me; I'm not that hungry."

"That's just no good!"

Surprisingly, Lucas was pretty angry at my response.

"We're here because we want to have lunch with you!"

His words struck me deeply.

…Yes, I was thinking about it too much…

"You mustn't waste the food your sister prepared!"

…Yes, I was simply thinking about it too much.

Though my second thought was almost identical to my first, the meaning was completely different. All I could do was sigh and take out my lunchbox. The trio's eyes were fixed entirely on the mysterious…contents. I already had a vague idea of what was inside…

I slowly and dramatically lifted the lunchbox lid as if I were a magician preparing the climax of his magic trick. The three swallowed in unison.

Clearly amused, I stopped teasing them and raised the lid all at once. What they saw was…

"…Vegetables?"

…as I expected.

"Carrots, cauliflower, broccoli, arugula, apple and orange slices… Are you a vegetarian?"

At Lucas's painful question, I bet I had a few tears in my eyes.

"Let's just say that I like my fruit and veg…"

As if grasping my situation, Mark tried to change the subject.

"By the way, how are things in your new class?"

I sighed deeply, trying to avoid banging my head against the table and shouting, 'Why did you ask that?!' Catching Rachael's aggressive gaze, Mark quickly noticed his mistake. Surely Rachael knew very well the situation that I was in.

"Um… Did I hit a sore spot?"

"Only a little…"

With a smile that was clearly half-forced, I could only come up with that as an answer to Mark's question.

"You can't help it, since there's a certain rivalry between the elements…"

Rachael's explanation seemed to kill the discussion, but Lucas's brilliant(?) wit soon gave it new life:

"One thing… You now have two uniforms, right?"

His question made sense, seeing as I now wore the brown diamond-shaped emblem.

"No. When they confirmed my elemental transfer, they took away my Water emblem and gave me the Earth one instead."

Rachael added to my explanation:

"Though the emblem looks like it's a part of the uniform, it is not. This makes it easier to change the emblem as the years go by. There are also budgetary reasons, but that's a separate matter."

"But isn't there a risk of someone pretending to be another year or another element to bypass restrictions?"

Mark had a fair point. However, this did not shake Rachael's explanation:

"There is no such problem. All necessary checks are carried out by academic representatives, so it's impossible to use an emblem other than the one assigned."

"Oh, that reminds me..."

Listening to the not-so-secret informant, I remembered what I really needed to know.

"...Rachael, can you tell me the situation with Earth?"

"Didn't the headmaster say anything to you?"

"Well, you see..."

And so, I explained the current situation—how the Guardian Spirit had his eyes on me, the headmaster's great expectations, and how I was a victim of all that.

"You poor thing..."

Lucas's words were full of compassion. Perhaps he'd had some similar experiences with his sister?

"No need to console me."

Rachael responded:

"Anyway, why are you curious about the current situation with Earth? Didn't you say you wouldn't become its representative?"

Even though I had already expressed my reluctance, it seemed like I was poking my nose where it didn't belong. I certainly had no sense of duty or attachment to this element, and I didn't have any quests related to it to complete, either. Although the Guardian Spirit and the headmaster had high expectations from me, I certainly had no obligation to meet those expectations.

...But one thing kept echoing in my head.

"...Save Earth."

I shook my head, trying to forget it. I had come to this academy for only one reason, and I didn't have time for anything else.

"Right now, I just want to assess the situation. I dislike not knowing what's happening around me."

Rachael carefully analyzed my answer and nodded her head.

"All right. I'm going to give you a summary; is that okay?"

"As long as you touch on all of the main points. I'll ask you to elaborate if I think it's necessary."

That said, I took out my notebook and opened it to a blank page. The other visible page was so messy that when Lucas saw it, he asked me what was written on it.

"They're notes."

Rachael's and Mark's curiosities were also piqued by my notebook, so I had no choice but to show them.

"They're scribbles…"

"I can't understand anything…"

In response to their criticism, I felt the need to give a 'You're right.' I then resumed the original topic:

"Firstly, could you please give me an introduction to the role of academic representatives?"

When she heard my preferred starting point, Rachael made a doubtful expression.

"Shouldn't you know that by now?"

"I'd like to hear your version, too."

"…All right."

After fixing her invisible glasses and changing her tone of voice, she went into 'professional mode.'

"First of all, the academic representatives are five students, one for each element, each chosen by the Guardian Spirit of their element to mediate between students and professors."

"So they won't use the no-confidence system?"

At Mark's question, Rachael nodded.

"First of all, that system was established for extreme cases where professors didn't want to discuss a particular topic with the students. The last time it was used was almost fifty years ago."

"So long ago, even though it's such a convenient system?"

Upon hearing her brother's voice, Rachael lost composure and began to sigh deeply.

"What did I ask wrong?!"

"The no-confidence system can only be used once every two months, and during that time, professors can issue as many changes as they want without students being able to protest."

"That's practically tyranny!"

"That's why it's only used in extreme cases. Let's just say it's the last resort before they use more forceful methods."

Grasping the hidden message, both Lucas and Mark fell silent.

The reason was quite simple, and we all had the same question in our heads:

Does that mean there was a student revolt?

Interesting though the subject may be, this was not why I had started the discussion.

"The no-confidence system is used not only for general issues but also for more specific situations. For example, suppose there is a problem concerning Fire. In this case, only Fire students would be involved in the no-confidence system. It makes them helpless if any further issues within their element occur over the next two months, but this does not mean that they are excluded from matters concerning the entire academy."

Rachael tried to continue her explanation, but I interrupted her:

"There's an inconsistency between what you just said and what my sister told me."

"An inconsistency?"

Rachael was evidently very curious about what I was referring to.

"You said that representatives are chosen by the Guardian Spirits... However, my sister said that representatives are chosen by their immediate predecessors; something doesn't add up."

Rachael grimaced. There was a short pause before she continued.

"...Because the Guardian Spirits don't care who their representatives are."

Mark, Lucas, and I were so shocked that you could clearly see it on our faces.

"...Just because they are the Guardian Spirits of the kingdom and have their sense of duty to guide their representatives does not mean that they approve of their representatives as 'true' chosen ones."

Having anticipated our obvious confusion, Rachael resumed her explanation:

"Guardian Spirits are beings that have lived long lives and therefore have high standards in the choice of their respective representatives. Unfortunately, over time, fewer and fewer students were able to meet these high standards, so the Guardian Spirits eventually became negligent in their selections."

Rachael looked me straight in the eye.

"That's why it's amazing that a Guardian Spirit specifically asked for a student."

Sensing my uniquely privileged situation, Mark and Lucas looked at me, surprised.

I...hate this feeling.

To shake the sense of discomfort from my body, I drew a quick doodle on the notebook, before asking another question:

"So that's why the Guardian Spirits have never been seen in public in recent years?"

Mark's and Lucas's puzzled expressions contrasted with Rachael's surprised expression. She quickly responded:

"You really know some strange info, don't you?"

With a simple laugh, I erased the newly tense atmosphere.

"On the first day of class, my sister told me that she had never seen the Guardian Spirit of Earth in person. On the day of the appointment, only he appeared of his own free will, whereas it seemed that the other Guardian Spirits were practically dragged out into the open."

Nodding at my explanation, Rachael gave further details:

"Since the Guardian Spirits had lost interest in academic affairs, they began only showing themselves to their representatives, and only teaching them the bare minimum for them to be able to perform their duty as academic representatives, at that."

"I've heard that sometimes the Guardian Spirit of Earth has completely ignored his representative for the whole year."

"Is he an idiot?"

At Mark's information and Lucas's impolite remark, Rachael couldn't help but give a strained smile.

"I can't blame him, after the...*decadence* of certain Earth representatives..."

Decadence, huh...

It seemed I had finally come to the heart of the matter—what I had to save Earth from.

"What is this...decadence?"

Rachael gave a heavy sigh.

"The reason is as stupid as it is real... Do you *really* want to know?"

I nodded my head.

"I want to know why I got caught up in all this."

Sighing again, Rachael met my gaze as she resigned herself to reveal the truth.

"...Harem."

...Huh...?

All the tension in my shoulders disappeared as if by magic, and the pen in my hand slipped and fell.

Harem…?

"What the hell is that supposed to mean?!"

I rose, scratching my head in perplexity. I was sure that the three of them were looking at me, but they certainly couldn't blame me. I thought that I'd find something dire like a curse or some secret cult manipulating the academy from the shadows, but instead…

"I told you the reason was stupid."

Rachael sighed yet again.

"In the last twenty years, the Earth representatives have been interested in the title because of the privileges it grants and the private time they get to spend with the other representatives. And, needless to say, all academic representatives of Fire, Water, Wind, and Lightning have been girls."

I could only lower my head and slump back down into my chair, devoid of energy.

"Basically, I'm supposed to stop this—this *womanizer dynasty?*"

What a pointless reason. I frowned.

"They might as well be left without a representative."

"They can't."

Rachael's immediate interjection piqued my interest.

"What makes you say that?"

"Without a representative to mediate with the kingdom, the entire element would fall apart. All areas assigned to the element would become abandoned, and its students would become a laughing stock for being so disorganized that they didn't even have a leader."

…Why me?

That was all I could think of in response. Rachael smiled.

"The Guardian Spirit of Earth didn't choose you to end the womanizer dynasty…or rather, that's not *all* he wants of you."

Looking at her expression, I couldn't see any signs of falsehood.

"I think he saw real potential in you and wants to cultivate your talent."

Both Mark and Lucas added genuine encouragement:

"I think so too."

"You stood toe to toe with a prospective representative during your duel, after all!"

…I really didn't know what to do in a situation like this. However, there was one thing that I did not forget:

"Thank you."

"I guess that's it!"

As if to signify the end of her explanation, Rachael spoke energetically.

"I don't know what you're going to do, but I hope I was at least a bit helpful."

Even though I was still at the starting point, I now had a clear view of my surroundings.

"You were, without a doubt."

Mark chimed in:

"So, what will you do now?"

My body instinctively took another notebook and began writing on it. The trio's eyes looked toward me. Turning the notebook sideways, I summarized Rachael's explanation at the top of the page.

"First of all, I found out what the headmaster wants Earth to be saved from, but I still don't know why the Guardian Spirit of Earth is so obsessed with me."

I used several arrows to link each question to its answer. With the exception of the gutter, I used all space available to write down everything I could...more legibly, this time. I was concentrating too hard to know what the three of them were doing, but in any case, it took me approximately five minutes to complete my work.

"...Even if I wanted to do something, I don't know where to begin. So...right now, I'll see how things develop."

When I stopped writing, I heard three sighs of admiration.

"T-this..."

"I don't believe it..."

"Did you summarize...everything we discussed?"

Lucas and Mark were staring intently at the notebook while Rachael asked how I did it.

"It's not that difficult; I took notes first."

"Ah..."

All three finally realized the merit of my earlier scribbles.

"Firstly, you take notes to remember the important points of a topic. Then, you can calmly revise them and highlight what's truly crucial."

"What a difference..."

"It doesn't look like these two notebooks belong to the same person..."

In response to Lucas's and Mark's amazement, all I could do was giggle.

"My sister often tells me that, too."

"Hmm?"

Noticing something, Rachael swiped the second notebook from the boys.

"Are these…notes for the lessons that are coming up in a few months?"

""Huh?""

Both Lucas and Mark wanted to see what Rachael was talking about.

"Hey, isn't this our element's coursework?"

"There's so much written for Earth, too…and so clearly!"

"I had prepared in advance, but it seems to have been in vain. Now I'm trying to get ahead of the current coursework."

Lucas was trying to grab hold of the notebook as soon as humanly possible. Mark was trying his best to restrain him, but it was clear that he, too, was attracted to it.

"Go ahead."

With my permission, they both took out notebooks to copy the whole thing.

"But you should study a little on your own, too. These are notes for me; there may be some things that you won't understand."

""Copy that!""

Rachael and I warmly watched over this amusing scene.

Maybe life at the academy isn't so bad, after all.

009: A Glimpse of the Truth

"Hold it right there!"

It was a typical day, just about time for the lunch break, and I was on my way to the former Astronomy Club room. Unfortunately, however, the day would not remain typical for long, as the haughty and immediately recognizable voice that had just called out to me demonstrated…

I reluctantly stopped in the middle of my walk through one of the open corridors of the academy that contained recreational space. Before turning around, I sighed, steeling myself.

I knew this moment would come sooner or later…

"What might the next Earth representative want from me?"

Seemingly pleased to hear my words, the owner of the voice gave a proud greeting:

"That is correct. It is I, Phillip Royals, the *next* representative of Earth."

For some reason, he put some emphasis on 'next,' but I ignored him. Three other Earth students, perhaps his lackeys, followed him. One of their faces was surprisingly familiar to me; it was the boy in my new class with dazzling straw-colored hair.

He seems to be one of Phillip's closest subordinates.

Reflecting on my memories of the first day after my class transfer, I could not help but give a sigh of resignation. The two lackeys whom I did not know began to criticize my behavior:

"What do you think you are doing in front of our representative?!"

"Have some manners!"

And what am I supposed to make of your manners…?

Keeping my complaints to myself, I tried to ignore them. Surprisingly, Phillip calmed them down with a magnanimous wave of his hand.

"There's no need for that. It is the privilege of the strong to let minor slights such as these go, especially if they come from a pitiful country bumpkin."

"…"

Phillip's claim was so absurd that it left me speechless, yet the two lackeys who had been silenced seemed to shower him with praise that my ears did not care to register.

"In any case…"

Phillip's following words made me remember that he had called out to me for a reason.

"…what are your true intentions?"

"Huh?"

I had no idea what he was talking about.

"Don't play dumb. There must be a reason why you are aiming for the title of representative."

I now understood what he meant.

"Do you mean to say that I have allied myself with the Guardian Spirit of Earth for a specific motive?"

"Of course."

I recognized the look in front of me; what he was searching for was not the truth but the distorted reality in which he believed. It would be a waste of time to even attempt to reason with him…

"What's up? Is someone *afraid*?"

"It's useless to try to stall for time!"

…and the other two seemed unwilling to listen, either. Since they weren't going to let me go so easily, I figured that I may as well extract some information from them.

Especially about Phillip.

I turned my gaze toward the only one who had remained quiet since the beginning of the discussion.

"You—with the straw-colored hair."

"…! What…is it?"

Although he was trying to appear calm, he was clearly somewhat shaken. It seemed that the first impression I had given him was still quite vivid in his mind… Unfortunately for him, I would not let him go so easily.

"What is your name?"

He looked around as if seeking approval from someone. Phillip did not stop him.

"…Ferdinand Ascalis."

It was the student who had tried to save me on my first day in my new class.

"Tell me…why is it that you follow Phillip?"

His behavior was clearly at odds with Phillip's.

"What kind of question is that?"

"Is it not obvious?!"

Those two were really getting on my nerves, interrupting me at every chance… With a gesture, Phillip ordered them to keep quiet and let Ferdinand speak. Before voicing his opinion, Ferdinand took a moment to breathe.

"Phillip is an exemplary role model to which all students in our element should aspire, from his diligent behavior in class to the excellent composure he exudes during missions."

Perfect.

Everything was going in the direction that I had planned. I would have liked to dig deeper, but I needed to seize this opportunity; after all, when you describe a person, you start from their positive aspects, especially their outward appearance.

And this is precisely where I aimed to strike.

"But what about his behavior outside of academics?"

"And just what do you mean by that?"

Naturally, Phillip intervened. I then shifted my gaze from Ferdinand to my *real* target.

"I've heard much talk about your…*numerous* romantic encounters."

Before the two irritating lackeys could open their mouths again, Phillip raised his hand casually to stop them, replying in a calm tone:

"Ah, you mean those rumors? Naturally, they are untrue."

Contrasting with the casual manner with which he had raised his hand, his tone and expression betrayed his great annoyance; he seemed to have answered this question innumerable times.

"Oh, if only you knew how many students are trying to ruin my image…but one as ordinary as you could scarcely comprehend the struggles of the popular. Sometimes, I almost envy the easy life you have lived, ha!"

…Easy?

While the two lackeys behind him were heartily laughing at Phillip's joke, I struggled with emotions that threatened to burst forth. I gritted my teeth. Only after lowering myself slightly and forcefully clenching my fists was I able to avoid succumbing to the urge to attack him.

"Hey, what the…"

"Answer me."

This was no time to mince words. Ferdinand seemed frightened by the serious tone that I had inadvertently used, but the others didn't seem to care.

"Why are these rumors about you running wild?"

"Why? Isn't it obvious that they're—"

"My sister."

Phillip stopped mid-sentence.

"I received confirmation from my sister that you are courting her."

"Your…sister?"

He seemed completely unaware of whom I was talking about. After a pause, he appeared to finally grasp the situation.

"Now that I think about it, someone does come to mind… The girl's surname… Anion, was it?"

His genuine ignorance of whom I was talking about was clear. It made my blood boil.

"Ah, now I remember. You're talking about Marie, the second-year in Water, no?"

His carefree tone was beginning to grate on my nerves. Just before I moved to intervene, he continued:

"This is all a misunderstanding. I am not courting her."

I certainly wasn't expecting *that*. After a few moments of amazement, my anger faded away almost as quickly as it had arisen. It was all a misunderstanding. My sister wasn't being bothered by this guy for *that* reason. I still didn't know why, but…

…Why do I feel so relieved?

Have I not been searching for someone to look after her?

Someone who can break our bond?

Perhaps…

I shook my head.

No. I just don't want someone like Phillip *by her side.*

Convinced, I ceased my inner reflection.

"Does that mean…?"

"That's right."

Without even letting me finish my question, he had already drawn his conclusion.

"This is all special training."

"…Huh…?"

Phillip continued his explanation, indifferent to the astonishment that was writ large upon my face:

"Isn't it obvious that an academic representative should have reliable supporters at his side? And what better than supporters whom he has *personally* trained?"

"…"

I was speechless.

His expression was carefree, as if what he had just said were the most natural thing in the world. No one raised the question of what exactly was so 'obvious' about this. Had the situation truly reached the point where even common sense was eroded, as Domizio and the headmaster had feared?

With a dry throat, I asked my final question:

"So…all of those female students in the rumors…?"

"Of course. They are all apprentices who wish to support me as closely as possible. Naturally, it is the same for your sis—"

Before he could even finish his sentence, my body moved on its own.

…!

Only because I remembered *his* words, I hesitated slightly in my reflexive charge, allowing Philip to narrowly avoid my attack. The punch that I had furiously unleashed struck one of the hallway's supporting columns, and the ensuing shock wave sent Phillip rolling away a few meters. His followers were just far enough away to withstand the impact. The column cracked considerably, debris flying at nearby onlookers.

Cloaking himself in magical power, Phillip enhanced his physical abilities and received no damage…except perhaps to his image. The other students had been watching our discussion secretly, but after *that* display, they were no longer afraid to openly observe.

Phillip stood up and looked me straight in the eye, incandescent with rage.

"What were you trying to do?!"

Without even waiting for a reply, Phillip began to run toward me, clearly hostile. I was shaking—but not because I was nervous.

Just like in that *moment…*

I saw *that* scene for an instant.

Two people on the forest floor…

My sister crying…

And my hands…

I frantically tried to clear my thoughts.

I'm not like I was back then.

Though I wished it were a prayer, I repeated it as if it were a curse.

I need some time to pull myself together.

I turned my eyes in *his* direction. After all…

"Do you really want to do this in front of your element's Guardian Spirit, *next representative of Earth?*"

Hearing my words, Phillip hurriedly halted his advance, but his hostile attitude did not entirely disappear. He looked around, clearly not believing me, but no matter where he or the onlookers looked, they could not find that elusive lizard.

"You would dare to bluff in such a shameful manner?!"

Phillip's outburst was justified, and the onlookers were supporting him, but...

"I'm not bluffing. He really is here, you know?"

I glared menacingly at the wall. Everyone in the vicinity soon followed.

"Even you wouldn't keep hiding after all this ruckus, would you?"

"...And who exactly is the cause of this commotion?"

Responding to my provocation, a strange brown stain on the academy wall became more and more visible. By the time it had developed into a faint silhouette of a lizard, the Guardian Spirit's presence became clear to everyone. Phillip, as were all of the onlookers, was incredulous.

"I am the Guardian Spirit of Earth, Domizio."

After observing everyone's terrified faces, Domizio focused his gaze on me as if to say, 'Look what I have to do because of you...'

I returned his gaze with an indifferent one. As if in surrender, he announced what I had been waiting for:

"Simon, Phillip. Cease this meaningless squabble."

- Another point of view -

It was just business as usual, observing Simon. I could never have imagined that the situation would escalate to this extent.

After Phillip's not-so-surprising revelation, I had given up hope. I had known that such activity had been occurring for several years within the management of Earth, but there had not been anything that I could do about it. Or, rather, it was better to say that I had decided to do nothing.

As I watched this decadence year after year, my faith in humans slowly faded away. Bitter and disgusted, one day, I decided to abandon Earth. I knew not whether it was because of my choice, but the element became more corrupt and selfish from that day on.

It was not just the representatives; the attitude of the entire element was slowly changing. Even though it distressed me, I felt that, deep down, I was relieved. Or rather...

...It truly did end up as I imagined it would...

As was the case in times past, humans think only to please themselves. They have no second thoughts about discarding something important if they begin to seek something even more meaningful.

Just like what happened to him. *Even though he fought for them, the humans...*

However, before I could finish my wearied monologue, my curiosity was piqued by an unexpected action—I felt a strong wave of magical power. Trying to find the source, I immediately opened my eyes.

It was at that moment that I saw Simon's movement. Although I tried my best not to miss the timing as I had on that day, it was only thanks to a moment of hesitation that I saw that scene.

In the blink of an eye, Simon had crossed the meter that separated the two of them, and he was about to land an emotion-fueled fist right on Phillip's cheek. With a single glance, I could feel the raging river of emotions roiling within it.

It was anger...and sadness. For no real reason, a tear trickled down my cheek.

Why are you so like him...?

The attack missed its target, instead hitting a support column behind Phillip. Even though the entire academy was strengthened directly by the Guardian Spirits' magical power, the pillar was severely damaged.

There was no need to call a construction worker, since the building had self-repairing capabilities, but the pillar, spiderwebbed with cracks, was a sight to behold. Inside the academy buildings, there were a few areas in which fighting was permitted, but on very few occasions were the students able to cause visible damage to the structures.

In the past, in order to successfully break through a wall, an entire class had had to focus all of their magical power.

If I remember correctly, that was when the students revolt—

Realizing that I was going off topic, I looked up to see Phillip get to his feet, his expression filled with anger and nothing else.

"What were you trying to do?!"

I sighed when I saw that reaction. I noticed no trace of wonder nor of fear, confirming my suspicions.

He knows nothing about the structure of the buildings or their sturdiness.

As I thought about how far the minimum knowledge held by the Earth representative had fallen, I saw Simon's almost mocking expression. His eyes locked with mine.

I have a bad feeling about this…

With timing that seemed so perfect as to be a jinx, Simon said something that sent a shiver down my spine:

"Do you really want to do this in front of your element's Guardian Spirit, *next representative of Earth*?"

Phillip ended his hysterical advance and looked around.

"You would dare to bluff in such a shameful manner?!"

"I'm not bluffing. He really is here, you know?"

Turning his gaze toward me, he revealed my location to everyone, although they were still unable to see me.

"Even you wouldn't keep hiding after all this ruckus, would you?"

Since he had cornered me, I sighed. It would seem that I no longer had any choice but to please him.

"…And who exactly is the cause of this commotion?"

I undid my invisibility spell, making my form visible. To the amazement of the bystanders, I gathered all of their attention.

First of all, I'd better deal with this mess.

"I am the Guardian Spirit of Earth, Domizio."

With just that, I was able to bring back a moment of silence. I took the opportunity to curse the culprit behind this mess, but he seemed completely unfazed. I was dancing in the palm of his hand, but there was truly nothing else that I could do; I didn't want this situation to get worse, too.

"Simon, Phillip. Cease this meaningless squabble."

Simon breathed a sigh of relief, but Phillip seemed eager to protest:

"Not before I've paid him back!"

Just as Phillip was about to resume his charge, Simon bowed slightly.

"My apologies; I slipped."

It went without saying that that his tone was not in the least apologetic. Furthermore, even before Phillip could argue back, Simon had one last thing to say to him:

"Isn't it the *privilege* of the strong to let minor slights go, especially when they come from a *pitiful country bumpkin?*"

"...!"

Phillip seemed on the verge of casting a spell in response to Simon's mocking quotation of his words, but a straw-haired student stepped in to calm him down. In the meantime, Simon continued with his haughty attitude and turned his back on Phillip. I was struggling to contain my laughter.

Fortunately, the focus is not on me.

If the students saw me right now, they would believe that I favored Simon. There *would* have been a pinch of truth to that, though. Simon was proving to be a more and more interesting student.

If he were my representative...

However, even though that was my goal, I could not force him.

I had to find a way to make him accept the title of his own free will. Although I still had no concrete plan, I knew what I needed to do in this moment.

"Simon Anion and Phillip Royals..."

Noticing my tone, Simon looked at me seriously. Phillip was still angry, but he calmed down just enough to listen to me.

"...I command you—follow me, just the two of you."

"What do you want now?!"

"To select who will be the next representative of Earth."

At those words, Phillip became excited, forgetting about the current issue, whereas Simon displayed an expression of annoyance.

You may not like it, but I am going to give you a trial.

After all, I cannot let you escape after seeing the potential that you have just demonstrated.

***

"We have arrived at the Sanctuary of Earth."

After following Domizio down a long and tortuous staircase that began inside the academy, Phillip and I had arrived at an underground cave that was so vast that it seemed like it might even be larger than the arena in which we had dueled earlier. There, we lost ourselves in admiration of the luminescent flowers that adorned the glimmering walls and ceiling.

The faint glow from these plants, which absorbed nutrients from their roots and released a shining magical substance into the surroundings, ordinarily afforded one only a meager view of their dark environment. However, the sheer scale of this subterranean flower garden illuminated the entire enormous cavern with a brilliant cyan light.

"It is time. Here, the trial to determine which of you will become my element's next academic representative shall begin."

Hearing these words from the Guardian Spirit, both Phillip and I stopped our admiration of the scenery. Positioned on a round rock that seemed incongruous with this desolate terrain, the brown lizard explained the terms of the trial to us:

"Your goal is simple. At the end of this cave, there is an object guarded by my alter ego. All you have to do is retrieve it and place it on this rock within one week."

"Alter ego?"

How intriguing.

Domizio continued, noticing that his words had piqued my curiosity:

"This cave is essentially a part of me. I can sense everything that happens within it, and I can command magical summons to obstruct you. Of course, I will order them not to kill you—but that does not mean that you will not *wish for death* instead…"

I ignored the anxiety that I could feel radiating from my opponent.

"So this means that I can sit back and do nothing for the entire week, right?"

Phillip's air of anxiety rapidly shifted to one of fury, but I continued to ignore him.

"Certainly—if you would like to become my representative."

Phillip and I were stunned.

"Just like last time, the rewards for each participant are different. If Phillip wins, I will appoint him as my academic representative. If Simon wins, he will *not* become my academic representative, and I will stop trying to convince him… However, if neither of you can deliver the item, Simon will become my academic representative."

"What is this injustice?!"

Phillip's wrath was completely understandable. He had already *won* before, and yet the odds were stacked against him even now.

"Oh? Do you mean to say that you don't have confidence in your ability to win?"

Phillip had no choice but to bite his tongue and remain silent.

"Why are you so obsessed with me...?"

Domizio did not answer my question, instead responding with a single sentence:

"Even if you do not become my next academic representative, I wish to see the extent of your *true* determination at least once."

Hearing his words, I couldn't help but feel annoyed.

"...Forget about it. After what happened at the duel..."

"You certainly are a sore loser, bumpkin."

Phillip was smirking.

To fail to understand what I was referring to... I couldn't help but envy Phillip's ignorance.

Yes, I wish I were ignorant...

If only I had never known what I really was...

No—one day, I would have found out anyway. I should be glad that I was now no longer oblivious to my situation and could act accordingly.

And I owe it all to her...

I put my concerns aside and declared my stance:

"I won't play your games anymore, Domizio."

The Guardian Spirit stared into my eyes and seemed disappointed. He turned his gaze toward Phillip and asked in a clinical voice:

"And what about you? Do you accept?"

"Certainly!"

Excited, his face could be read like a book.

I recalled what Rachael had said to me a few days ago.

"...Harem..."

I whispered that single word into the slightly stale subterranean air, but Phillip did not notice. The same could not be said for the Guardian Spirit, who sighed deeply.

"...When you are ready, descend those stairs and explore the labyrinth. If fortune smiles upon you, you may reach your destination within two hours."

Domizio pointed toward the dark void on the left side of the cave, leading our eyes to a gargantuan staircase hewn out of the stone. Not even the glow from the grand flower garden could illuminate the depths of the abyss below.

"What's that door for?"

Phillip seemed frightened by the darkness, raising a question about the door that was located in the opposite direction.

"…Think nothing of it. It cannot be opened."

Sensing the deep sadness contained within Domizio's statement, I let my curiosity get the better of me and I asked for further details. With a painful expression, the lizard reluctantly explained:

"…That door leads to the destination that I was telling you about. However, the two of you will not be able to open it."

"You've got to be kidding me!"

Phillip raced to the door and tried to breach it. Domizio and I looked at each other with bitter expressions and slowly followed him.

When we caught up to him, Phillip had still failed to even scratch the door.

"Stupid door!"

He summoned numerous golem knights in an attempt to destroy it. However—

"It is no use."

As if the Guardian Spirit's words were a prophecy, the golems' swords snapped one after the other.

"As I said, this cave is like a part of me. Pitiful attacks like that won't even tickle."

Domizio's words annoyed Phillip, but he was right; such an attack was quite pathetic.

"So does that mean you can open the door?"

"That is incorrect."

Phillip was perplexed by the lizard's answer. Domizio's expression morphed into one of suffering once more.

"As I have already told you, this cave is like a part of me. However, that does not mean that it always obeys my commands. This door listens to my heart; it will not open until I find someone truly worthy of my respect."

I found myself…conflicted.

If I tried to open that door, would it let me?

If so, I could immediately end this charade and grant Phillip the victory.

But if it really opened…would that mean that I have the respect of a Guardian Spirit?

Noticing my concern, Domizio answered with a weary tone:

"You cannot open it."

"Huh?"

"Although it is true that I am curious about you, that is not the respect that I was talking about. Also…"

That intentionally halted sentence was rather suspicious, but it did not matter to me. I had no intention of becoming a representative or gaining the respect of a Guardian Spirit. I turned around and headed for the stairs.

Domizio said nothing, as did Phillip.

It won't be you who chooses my fate.

Without any hesitation, I ascended the stairs, heading to where an ordinary academic life awaited me.

***

A few days had passed.

No one knew how it had started, but the rumor that the selection of the Earth representative was underway had spread widely.

"Phillip challenged both the Guardian Spirit and the impostor."

"He valiantly wishes to save his element from tyranny."

"The impostor is lazing around, enjoying the protection of the Guardian Spirit."

These rumors and more had become the discussion topic of all kinds of students. They weren't exactly far from the truth, but in the end, they were just hearsay. As long as it was just verbal harassment, I could still take it. In fact, even if it were physical harassment, I was convinced that it wouldn't matter at all—unlike in the past, I had grown up. I had already experienced those trying times once before.

During the past few days, I had always been the target of my classmates' attention. It seemed that the respect they held for Phillip and the fact that they'd grown a bit used to the pressure that I was releasing had made them brave enough to make a small non-verbal protest. However, they still dared not speak to me directly and could only make ruthless comments from afar.

But that didn't matter to me. I would not budge, and even if I became an academic representative, I would either neglect my role or leave the academy.

I had no intention of becoming a soldier or magic researcher. The only reason I enrolled was my sister's stubbornness, and she would understand if I withdrew after things got out of control.

And yet…

I sighed deeply. I had a feeling that I would have to act soon. Because…

I had a hunch that Phillip would not succeed.

- Another point of view -

"Tell me…why is it that you follow Phillip?"

Several days had passed since that event. Phillip hadn't shown up to class, and everyone was convinced that he was trying to pass the trial set by the Guardian Spirit of Earth, while Simon…

"…"

The class was shrouded in a gloomy silence; only the diligent scribbling of a single pen could be heard. It wasn't that no one was present, though. Rather, no one dared to make a sound—not even the professor, who was breaking out in a cold sweat.

The cause of all this was Simon Anion.

After the sound of the bell, the professor was the first to leave the class. Although neither I nor any of my classmates had this freedom, fortunately, it was the bell that marked the beginning of break time. Simon left the class as usual, causing the gloomy atmosphere of the classroom to immediately dissipate.

"He's finally gone…"

"I can't take it anymore…"

"Nobody told me we'd have a demon in our class!"

The cries of my comrades made me remember the hostile look he had given us on his first day of class.

A demon…

That was the only way of describing him.

✳✳✳

Since Phillip never showed up again, the small group of students I was a part of that gathered under his command became unnecessary, so we decided to separate until further notice. I was grateful for this occasion.

Done with lessons for the day, I decided to move to the forest to train during my newly obtained free time. I could go to the arena or the practice grounds, but either way, I needed some time alone.

My head was practically spinning with confusion, and I didn't want to see anyone at the moment.

A cold gust of wind reminded me that the temperature would only drop from here on. Although not even a month had passed since the start of my academic life, the time I had spent in my hometown with my family now seemed like a distant memory.

Why...?

After rearranging my neck warmer so I wouldn't get sick, I unsheathed my catalysts and recited the already outdated chant for creating a golem.

That's right; outdated.

Creating a single golem was a basic spell that would soon be replaced by more advanced ones, such as strengthening one's defensive abilities until they were far superior to those of a simple golem—allowing for close-range combat—or instead summoning an entire army of golems for long-range battle. Each style had its own flaws, namely low range and high consumption of magical power, but at close range, Earth mages were practically unbeatable...

...except that actual fighting was pretty much only done from a distance.

While Fire mages were known for their sheer firepower, Water mages for both their utility in the medical arts and their piercing power, Wind mages for their ability to fly through the air, and Lightning mages for their ability to paralyze and disable others before they could even chant their spells, Earth mages currently didn't possess any particular trait to make up for their shortcomings.

Except for *him*.

Which is why I started following him.

Phillip had decided to focus entirely on the second style.

'If close-range combat is obsolete, commit to long-range combat instead.' It was a route that was debated by many and abandoned by many more, but in Phillip's hands...

"But what about his behavior outside of academics?"

"Tch..."

I lost focus, and the spell failed, causing an explosion...at least, that's what was supposed to happen. With the snap of a finger, the magical power that had gathered dispersed, and everything returned to normal.

The ability to undo spells before they were even cast was essential for anyone who wanted to join the military. After forcibly undoing a spell, the caster would suffer a severe impact to their magic circuit that could cause substantial injuries, but it was still preferable to fully casting a failed spell.

I don't mean to brag, but my ability to halt failed spells was unrivaled. However, objectively speaking, this skill was practically useless, since it served only to negate the careless mistakes I made—ideally, there should be no failures to begin with.

All students at this academy had worked hard to pass the entrance exams, and I was no different. Unlike the idiot who caused an explosion.

"…"

For some reason, all I could do was compare myself to that fool. Although Phillip was the perfect leader, the Guardian Spirit favored appointing an unheard-of student.

"That person is not suitable for—"

A knot in my throat prevented me from completing my sentence.

Why…?

I felt that Simon's actions were distinctly different from Phillip's. If Phillip's style was what I was looking for, then Simon's was….

A wave of strong nausea spread through my body, causing me to stagger. Only by leaning on the nearest tree was I able to regain my balance and shake off this bad feeling.

In an effort to better myself, I had decided to study under the most capable person in the academy. However…

Why are these rumors about you running wild?

"…"

I sighed and decided to call it a day. No matter how hard I tried, I could not stop thinking about that discussion, and being this distracted wouldn't lead to good results. Additionally, the gray clouds that covered the sky were a sign of an impending storm. Unlike my uniform, the neck warmer I was wearing was not magically coated to protect it from the environment, and I wanted to avoid ruining it.

As I was about to head back to my dorm, I heard female voices nearby. A female Water student was saying goodbye to two others.

"Leticia, Irene, I'll see you tomorrow."

"Have a safe trip home!"

"See you tomorrow, Marie!"

Marie…?

Where had I heard that name before?

"My sister."

So she was…

Unconsciously, I stealthily followed the chestnut-haired girl, weaving my way between the trees.

Why am I doing this…?

Before I could come up with an answer, my legs continued moving on their own.

…?

Something was strange—the Water dormitory wasn't in this direction. The only building in this direction was…

"How much longer do you intend to follow me?"

…! I've been discovered!

Confused, I didn't know what to do. Escape? Hide?

Wait a minute…

Why was I trying to avoid her? Convinced, I revealed myself.

"An Earth first-year…?"

Looking at the emblem on the breast of my uniform shirt, she seemed perplexed. Bowing, I introduced myself:

"Ferdinand Ascalis, first-year of Earth."

Mirroring the formality I showed, the girl in front of me also made a slight bow.

"Marie Anion, second-year of Water."

Anion… There is no doubt about it.

"Did you need something from me?"

I didn't know how to answer her. Why *was* I following her?

"This is all special training."

I gritted my teeth. It would haunt me for the rest of my life if I didn't ask her here…

"Is it true that you're undergoing…special training with Phillip?"

In response to my question, the girl became visibly exhausted.

"So that's how he sees it…"

This confirmed my doubt, and my image of Phillip began to crumble.

"Why…"

Clenching my fists, I could not contain my voice.

"Why is Phillip lying?!"

The girl seemed surprised.

"What reason could he have?!"

My thoughts seemed like they would spiral out of control and take my mind with them.

"Why do I have all these doubts?!"

Doubts that slowly gnawed at my soul.

"He was…my ideal! I…"

Before I knew it, the girl was standing in front of me. And…

She hugged me.

…!!

I tried to break free, but I was unsuccessful; she seemed strangely familiar with this situation.

"There is no guilt in feeling lost."

Her words made me lose the strength to resist.

"At the moment, you have only lost sight of the road ahead."

My fate—was literally in her hands.

"It's okay to take a break."

"…"

She spoke in a soothing voice, as if she were trying to heal all of the wounds that scarred my psyche. It was a warmth that I had already experienced, a warmth that was telling me to give in and share my suffering with another.

"Why…"

The girl named Marie didn't rush me.

"Why… Why is Phillip lying?!"

To demand answers from a stranger…I must have completely lost my mind.

"From the moment I first saw him in action, I had no doubt that his path was the right one. That if I followed him, I wouldn't be led astray. So…why…?"

Marie remained silent.

"Following his directions, I have…done many things. Some that I am truly proud of, while others… And Simon… I—"

For a moment, it seemed that the grip around my neck had tightened. Without even giving me time to think about what had just happened, the girl who was hugging me spoke:

"What did you do to my brother…?"

It was then that I remembered that I was standing in front of his sister. What should I do? Confess my sins and receive my punishment, or play dumb…?

But no matter how much I thought about it or how much time passed, Marie didn't loosen her grip or force me to speak.

I chose to give in.

"Under orders from Phillip, a group of students within his class has been tasked with sabotaging his academic life…"

"Why did he order you to harass my brother?"

"I…don't know."

My mind was in utter turmoil; I didn't notice the change in the tone of Marie's voice.

"I always thought that…things would never go wrong if I followed Phillip. Chasing the approval of others, forming secret alliances, and even resorting to subterfuge… As strange as it seemed to me, I thought this was what it meant to be strong."

After a few seconds of silence, I was asked a question:

"Why are you in such a rush?"

"In a…rush?"

I didn't know how to answer her.

"Chasing after someone else's footsteps is not a sign of growth—it's searching for a shortcut that will lead you to a dead end."

Marie did not mince words.

"As far as I know, he's always been an arrogant person."

An overwhelming impulse compelling me, I reached for her shoulders, pushed her aside, and yelled.

"You don't know his true worth!"

But Marie did not look away.

"Then, do *you*?"

I hesitated.

I… Do I really know Phillip?

"Can you say with certainty that the others are lying?"

Shut up.

"Can you say with certainty that the Phillip you know is the real Phillip?"

Shut up. Shut up.

"Can you say with certainty that Phillip would never do such things?"

Shut up. Shut up. Shut up!

"Or are you just ignoring the bad within Phillip and seeing only the good?"

"Then… WHAT AM I SUPPOSED TO *DO?!*"

I screamed as though I were using my very soul to fuel my lungs. I couldn't look her in the face anymore. Her questions weighed more and more heavily on my mind.

I had lost my way.

"Look at reality and never lose sight of it."

The girl approached me. Soon, I felt her warm embrace once more.

"Don't close your eyes to yourself.

"Don't look away from what it is that you are truly searching for.

"Don't look away from Phillip."

I repeated her words like a mantra, my mind racing to digest them.

"Don't…look away…?"

"It's still not too late for you."

"What do…"

Releasing me from her embrace, Marie turned around and walked away.

…you mean?

That is what I wanted to ask her, but catching a glimpse of her face as she turned around made me realize that I could not finish my sentence. What I saw was a grief-stricken expression that made my heart ache.

Without another word, the girl named Marie disappeared from my sight.

It wasn't until the rain began to fall that I was able to move again. Its biting chill only made the dying motes of Marie's warmth stand out even further, and the words that she had left me with never stopped echoing inside my head.

"Don't…look away…"

I didn't know what I wanted to do yet, but…

"It's okay to take a break."

010: Interlude—A Bath, Resolve, and a Meeting

"Damn it!"

It was a few minutes after the end of class, and I was on my way home…and a thunderstorm had just appeared. Unfortunately, I did not have an umbrella on me, so I had no choice but to run.

I opened the door to my apartment. No one was inside; I remembered that it had been a few days since my sister had assured me that she would spend more time with her friends. I was relieved to see that she was taking better care of herself, but that didn't make it any easier to ignore the loneliness that I felt.

Taking off my leather shoes, I noticed that I was soaked through. I sighed at the realization that I would have to do the laundry earlier than anticipated, then stepped back outside. Since the floor above shielded the entire connecting hallway from the weather, there was no need to worry about leaving my shoes here to dry.

After entering my apartment again—hopefully for longer this time—and closing the door, I briefly paused in amazement at how effective the anti-noise features of the building were. The roar of the pouring rain was completely absent inside. It was *too* quiet.

I sighed contemplatively. Taking off my socks to avoid slipping on the floor, I crossed the hallway and headed for the bathroom that was directly in front of me. I took off my clothes and placed them directly into the washing machine (they were all colors) then took two towels—one to dry myself and one to cover my lower half. If my sister…saw me like this, it would be quite unfortunate.

After turning on the faucet of the bath that was separated from the rest of the bathroom by a sliding door, I grabbed a rag to wipe the droplets of water that had fallen in the hallway. I then patted my shoes dry; being made of leather, they shouldn't be left out in the wind while still sopping wet.

I crumpled a few sheets of old newspaper to absorb the remaining moisture from inside the shoes, all the while feeling like I had forgotten something… I soon remembered to spread the rag at the entrance for my sister's return.

I returned to the bathroom and cleaned my body before diving into the tub, which was now full to the brim.

"Ahh…"

With a sigh that was longer than usual, I realized that I had accumulated more fatigue than I had thought. Between that meddling lizard, my subsequent class transfer, and the matter of the academic-representative selection, it was no wonder that I was exhausted.

In the middle of melting in tranquility within the warm water, I heard the sound of a door being opened.

"I'm back!"

I'd recognize that energetic voice anywhere.

"Welcome home!"

"Oh? Are you in the bath?"

I had no intention of budging from my sanctuary, so I had raised my voice slightly.

"Yeah, looks like I really needed one."

"Oh, really? Please take your time, then."

Ever the perfect sister, she noticed the hint of tiredness in my voice—the very tiredness that prevented me from predicting what was to come…

A few minutes later, just as I was about to get out of the water…

Creak!

The sound of a door opening.

"Wha…!"

"Coming through!"

Startled, I felt myself slipping back into the bathtub. I immediately resurfaced—spitting the water that I had nearly swallowed from my mouth—to the gentle rustle of clothing being removed.

"Wait! I'm still—"

"Big Sis is here to lend you a hand~"

"I'm not a baby!"

Ignoring my protests, my sister barged into the bathing area.

"In that case, young man, do allow me to offer to help wash your back, since you're so exhausted."

"What are you, my handmaid?!"

My eyes were shut tight; all I could do was verbally protest.

"Oh? Do you really want to kick out your sister, who just returned from out in the freezing rain and might just be on the verge of catching something?"

"You're the second-best Water student; I'd be surprised if something as simple as rain could even touch you! And our uniforms have temperature-regulation features, so you're even *less* likely to fall ill!"

"If you doubt my words, you're more than welcome to take a look."

Now that's just underhanded—saying that so casually!

Expressing my disagreement by rolling face down and blowing bubbles underwater, I heard the showerhead being turned on and the soft sound of droplets hitting flesh...

"Too late! Now you'll never know if I was telling the truth."

It's no use.

I could never win against my sister.

"I put all of my wet clothes in the washing machine!"

"Did you even bother to separate the colors from the whites...?"

"Hmph. I may not be able to work the machine, but I can at least do *that*!"

The sound of the droplets stopped, and I felt an object trailing through the water near me.

"I'll forgive you if you give me a hand with my hair~"

"Roger, roger..."

I opened my eyes, confirming my suspicion—the girl in front of me was wearing a swimsuit.

Proudly displaying her bare shoulders and thighs, this dark blue one-piece was the standard academy model, which female Water students generally wore during the specialized training trip that was held every year (other elements held similar training trips, but I digress). The wielder of that lethal weapon turned coyly over her shoulder to face me from her elegant position atop a small wooden stool, before turning back and offering me her luxuriant hair.

"You could have told me that you were wearing your swimsuit..."

"Oh, my! Could it be that my innocent little brother was imagining something else?"

"Tch..."

The one saving grace was that our gazes couldn't cross at the moment, so she wouldn't be able to see my mortified expression.

With a devilish grin (I imagine), my sister proffered the showerhead. Accepting it with a smirk of my own, I began to wet her hair at full blast from directly above.

"Careful! That's a woman's treasure you're handling, you know?"

"Vengeance is mine!"

I smoothly decreased the intensity of the water, the flow fading to a gentle caress. My sister's mood soon improved, and she began to hum, her eyes happily closed.

"I haven't heard that tune before."

"Yes, it's quite new. The beat is so bizarre, but it's somehow still catchy—in fact, it could even be the opening of this series!"

"Hey, you're jinxing it!"

Our merry laughter resounded through the bathing area. I lowered the showerhead to grab the shampoo and began to slowly and carefully wash my sister's long hair as she resumed her humming. The lavender scent of the shampoo pervaded the room, strangely sweeter than before.

All was well at last.

"Marie, tell me…"

"Mm?"

"What happened on the way home?"

My sister remained silent.

The fact that she had entered the bathroom with me, the fact that she had mostly avoided showing me her face, and this attitude that made it seem like she was seeking my attention…

"Did something happen that made you remember the past?"

My sister let out a long sigh before admitting it.

"And I did my best to hide it, too…"

"How long have we known each other?! You tried so hard to distract me, but all I needed was the brief moment that you looked over your shoulder while trying to charm me to know that something was up."

"You got me there… But is it really *that* strange that I want to be spoiled by my brother?"

"Careful, now; there are some who would start saying strange things about you…"

"Says the person who claims to really, *really* love his sis—"

"Completely different."

I was trying my best to fight this…disease, but that seemed like a war that I had poor prospects of winning.

After I finished soaping her hair, I picked up the showerhead to rinse her off. Only the splashing of water could be heard in the bathroom as my sister began to tell me her concerns.

"I met a classmate of yours. His name was Ferdinand."

It took me a while, but I eventually remembered who he was. I still wondered why someone like him would follow Phillip…

"He seems to have lost his way… Looking for something, I mean."

"Ah—"

The showerhead slipped out of my hand, sinking into the bathtub.

"I did my best to encourage him, but in the end, he will have to make a choice: chase perfection or accept reality. The same choice I had to make..."

The delicate figure of my sister seemed to tremble before my very eyes. My instincts told me to reassure her, but my mind said that I had no right; empty words were all that came out of my mouth.

"For the moment, I am right here, beside you."

"...For the moment..."

My chest tightened as my sister repeated what I had just told her.

***

After fully rinsing my sister's hair, I had left the bathroom at the first possible opportunity. She had willingly chosen to not press any further, and I was grateful for that —if she had seen me in this condition, she would have put on a false smile to try to cheer me up. And I didn't want that.

I started the washing machine and dressed myself in comfortable clothing, before preparing dinner. When I laid everything out on the dining table, my sister showed up in the living room as if our conversation in the bathroom had never happened. After the meal, we both stayed in the living room to complete some homework for tomorrow's classes before going to bed.

Our apartment's bedroom was directly across from the living room and adjacent to the bathroom. As my sister crossed the hallway to enter it, I headed to the bathroom to retrieve our uniforms from the washing machine and put them on the rack to dry. When I returned, my sister was waiting for me, dressed in light blue pajamas that highlighted her womanly charms. As she sat on the bottom bunk of the bunk bed that we shared, she tied her hair to the side with a yellow butterfly-shaped hair tie so that she would not ruin it in her sleep.

She's still doing it...

"You know you don't have to wai—"

"I'm not straining myself; I just want to do this for my dear brother."

I wanted to rebuke her, for last time, she had waited for me until she was literally collapsing from sleep, but tonight was different—I could still sense a hint of insecurity within her voice. Sighing, I got changed as well (not minding my sister's gaze) and sat down next to her.

All that could be heard was her bunk bed's creaks of protest at the unexpected additional weight.

After a moment that seemed like an eternity, my sister broke the silence.

"Your body… It's fine, right?"

She was clearly referring to the fact that I had still been covered in bandages until a few days ago.

"As fine as fine can be—you know that better than I do. And…I must say, after unleashing some magical power against Phillip, my body is recovering even faster."

My sister held my arm close to her chest, transmitting her warmth.

"…Thank you."

"There is nothing to thank me for."

Hiding that I had gotten angry for her sake would be useless; she could read me like a book.

Neither of us spoke in this silent world. There was no need for words—our skin transmitted all that was needed.

***

I didn't know how much time had passed, but my sister eventually fell asleep, a smile on her lips. Trying my best not to wake her up, I placed her under her blankets so that she wouldn't catch a cold.

"Good night, Marie."

Against my expectations, however, I found my arm held hostage, enveloped in a pillowy warmth. Completely caught off guard, I struggled to break free, but it was no use —Marie simply tightened her grip even further.

Looks like I have no other choice…

I moved closer to her…

Looks like I have no other choice…

I moved closer to her…

…our faces almost touched…

And—

"Achoo!"

I hurriedly removed my cowlick from her nose and broke free, only pausing to wipe the sweat from my forehead when I had fully escaped her clutches. I gazed softly at her face, a smile naturally forming on my lips.

My sister was a klutz—a side of her that she revealed only to me. To everyone else, she was a model student, admired by even the Water representative.

…!

A sharp pain stabbed my core. I knew the reason; I just ignored it. The ache was intense, but it left as quickly as it came.

With one last look at my sister's face, I climbed the ladder and lay down.

***

Evidently, the long bath had not made my fatigue fade entirely, for I fell asleep almost immediately. Before I knew it, sunlight filtered through the frosted window that led to the connecting hallway, rousing me.

Looks like it's going to be sunny today.

I descended the bunk-bed ladder. It seemed like my sister hadn't woken up on time today, either.

"Marie, time to wake up."

"Mm…"

Reaching over to shake her shoulders, I found myself the victim of a sudden hug. I resigned myself to this stubborn sleeping habit of hers, my head resting on her chest.

"Marie…"

"Don't leave me all alone…"

…!

The joyful atmosphere from last night shattered like glass.

I can't let this continue.

The pain in my chest came back, stronger this time. My harsh reality returned, and I thought back to the past. It was inevitable that I would think back to *that* situation…

The situation I caused.

Gritting my teeth, I renewed my resolve.

Marie, I hope you find it during your time at this academy…

Something to make it less bitter—when our inevitable separation comes.

Meanwhile, in the underground cave…

"I-impossible!"

One by one, the many glorious knights that I summoned were crushed like insects.

"How can I defeat such a monster…?"

Faced with a creature I had never seen before, I found my path blocked. Although I could more or less see my target, the distance to it seemed insurmountable.

"Ah…!"

It was at that moment that I noticed my naivete.

"To get…*him* appointed as representative, that lizard is capable of playing dirty."

This was no time to hold myself back.

"Two can play at that game…"

I turned around, headed for the academy…

- Another point of view -

I knocked on the door in front of me.

"Enter."

I opened the door and spotted a familiar—*too* familiar—third-year student with a smug grin on his face. Phillip Royals awaited me on an ornate armchair, resting his feet on the pristine wooden table. After glancing at my face, he nodded.

"I am glad that you accepted my invitation."

I was utterly speechless.

"…Did you get permission to use this room?"

The room we were in was no ordinary space; it was the room reserved for the Earth representative…which Phillip was not.

"It will be mine before long; what difference does it make? Naturally, the students who carried my belongings here are of the same opinion."

How shameless! Where did all this confidence come from?!

I ceased all logical reasoning; it would be a waste of energy to even reply. Interpreting my lack of protest as agreement, Phillip stood up and invited me to sit on one of the guest chairs. To my surprise, he offered me tea and sat across from me. Since I had accepted his invitation, I had no choice but to take a sip.

"Is the tea to your liking?"

"Did you *seriously* summon me here to rate your brewing skills?"

Phillip was not flustered and continued in an unnervingly friendly tone:

"A bit of small talk never hurt anyone, no?"

I put my cup on the table at the maximum socially acceptable speed.

"If you have nothing else to discuss, I'm leaving."

Undeterred by my slightly raised voice, Phillip finally moved to the main topic:

"Come, now; there's no need to be so upset. After all, we're here for a *little chat* about *your brother*, Marie."

"That's why I'm here. I would never have shared a room with you otherwise."

"Anyway, I'm glad you accepted. I've invited you countless times, but you always refuse—what a wonderful sibling bond the two of you must have!"

Something's not right.

135

Phillip was acting too strangely. He was the type to easily fall for taunts…this charade was all too obvious.

"Spare me the pretense—what do you want with my brother?"

"I simply want to know your opinion about him being a candidate for the position of Earth representative."

"…"

I just couldn't figure out what he was planning. Figuring that it was best to get along for the time being, I answered honestly:

"I don't think he's suited to the role at the moment."

"Oh?"

Phillip's genuine expression of surprise was immediately replaced by a puzzled one.

"Now *this* is a surprise. What happened to your wonderful sibling bond?"

I bit my lip to hold back the anger I was feeling—but also to hide the immense frustration that had been tormenting me for some time. I wanted to slap him, and one other, so badly…

It took me a few seconds to calm down enough to think of how to respond.

"…I'd say he doesn't have enough experience in communicating with others."

"That's it?"

…I just didn't know what the point of all of this was; if he wanted to discover a weakness of Simon's, these questions were useless.

"…He also lacks self-awareness and the ability to fairly assess himself."

"Fairly assess himself?"

"That is correct. He values himself as far less than what he's truly worth, which prevents him from making the right decisions."

Phillip erupted into raucous laughter.

"So you think he's worth more than a gnat?"

I leaped to my feet in anger—but my legs gave out from underneath me. My vision fading, I fought to keep my eyes open…

"Why…?"

I fell. I couldn't lift a finger.

"Foolish gnats need to learn their place. And with your…*cooperation*, everyone will see the rise of a *true* academic representative!"

Witnessing Phillip's descent into madness, I fell into a deep, deep sleep…

011: The Trial

Toward the end of the break, I returned to class to find some people leaning over my desk. It was Ferdinand and Phillip's two lackeys. I wanted to ignore them, but they approached me.

"Hey!"

"Don't ignore us!"

"…"

"?"

I noticed that Ferdinand was behaving strangely, but because the two lackeys were being noisy, I didn't have time to think about it.

"We're here on behalf of Phillip!"

"It's a matter that concerns you, hehehe."

With them speaking so loudly, it was inevitable that the entire class turned to look; I didn't like their expressions at all. All they did was remind me of the faces of *those* two.

And the atrocity that I committed.

I took a deep breath and began to think. If Phillip was looking for me, he probably wanted either to shove his victory in my face or to ask me to retrieve the key object in his stead…but given the size of his ego, I doubted that it was the former. If he had already recovered the item, he would no doubt have made an announcement to the entire academy; surely he of all people would gloat over his victory, which would crown him the true Earth representative?

As for the latter case, there were two possibilities: either it was a sign of Phillip's incompetence, or…there was something sinister afoot.

That's when I realized where the issue lay—incompetent though he may be, Phillip was still the best Earth student in the academy, able to use four catalysts simultaneously. If such a person was unable to complete a mission within the academy grounds, it could mean only one thing: the task was too difficult.

Even that lizard should be able to restrain himself…

In any case, I decided not to act. I tried to sit at my desk, since I wasn't interested, but they held me in place by the shoulders, snickering in unison in my ears:

"Your sister's waiting for you, too."

My body froze.

"…What does that mean?"

Realizing that they had my attention, their expressions changed. I recognized those looks; they were full of wickedness and malice.

"Who knows?"

"We wanted to tell you, but…"

Realizing that they had the upper hand, they did their best to make me suffer as much as they could. I couldn't help but regret my behavior, for getting my classmates to hate me hadn't make my life any easier.

All I could do was curse myself.

"…Could I know what Phillip's message was…please?"

My voice was hoarser than ever before. I hated doing the bidding of others; lend them a helping hand and they'll want the whole arm next.

"We'll tell you, of course—if you prostrate yourself and beg!"

I wanted to punch someone. No, make that more than one.

The classmates who understood what was going on were laughing. Surrounding me, they released all of the stress that they accumulated over the past few days.

I wanted to run away. I hated being stared at in this way.

But I couldn't.

I got down on my knees and pressed my forehead into the ground. I couldn't help but swallow before I said what came next.

"Please, this foolish gnat implores you: might one as lowly as I hope to know what it is that the almighty Phillip desires of him?"

Two laughs could be heard from above where I lay prostrate. Soon, countless others followed from behind me.

"Yes, yes! That's right; you're a gnat, and Phillip is almighty!"

"A gnat like you should be thankful that Phillip is gracious enough to spend even a second of his valuable time on you!"

I was imprisoned in a cage of mocking laugher.

I wanted to flee, but I could not.

I wanted to hide, but I could not.

I wanted to die, *but I could not do even that.*

My sister—*was more important than my very life.*

I was prepared to discard everything I owned for her sake. Dignity, freedom, even my life itself… I would sacrifice anything and everything if it were for the sake of my sister.

I did not have the *right* to hesitate. However—

Someone gently pulled me to my feet by my arm.

"Phillip is waiting for you in the Sanctuary of Earth…together with your sister."

I recognized this voice—it was Ferdinand Ascalis. I couldn't see the look on his face, but the tone of his voice didn't contain even a hint of disdain. Ignoring the students who were annoyed that he was spoiling their fun, he strengthened his grip encouragingly.

"You'd better hurry."

Without giving him a response, I freed myself from his grip and ran for the cave as quickly as I could.

No…

Perhaps it is the class *that I am truly trying to flee.*

The looks of those who watched my flight were full of enmity and arrogance.

Although I was moving away from them, each step I took was heavier than the last. I stopped to check my condition; my cold hands shook uncontrollably, lacking warmth.

Huh?

Why was my vision…blurred? I rubbed my eyes and felt something formless.

"Ah…"

I was crying. Realizing what was happening, I quickly tried to dry my tears, but it was useless.

Marie…!

I sprinted toward the cave, my mind racing; I had to get there quickly, but it was foolish to go without a plan.

When I realized what it was that I had to do, my tears stopped falling.

"Two can play at that game…"

I'm not proud of using this method, but it looks like I have no other choice.

I ran even faster.

✱✱✱

"Took you long enough."

"I'm sorry; I didn't remember the way."

After descending the final stair, I entered the Sanctuary of Earth. In the middle of the room, there were two people: Phillip Royals and...

"What have you done to my sister?!"

Behind Phillip, my sister lay motionless on the ground.

No matter how strong he was, there was no way that Phillip could have bested her in a fair fight...

I tried to get closer, but Phillip effortlessly drew a magic circle. A golem knight appeared, restraining Marie with one arm and holding a pointlessly large sword to her throat with the other.

"I wouldn't do that if I were you."

He gloated, clearly enjoying the situation. I reluctantly suppressed the anger within me and extended a hand downward in a meaningful gesture.

"What do you want from me?"

"It's simple: fetch the object that lizard wants...and give it to me."

Just as I thought.

"You mean to tell me the vaunted academic representative of Earth is incapable of accomplishing such a simple task?"

"Shut up!"

He was visibly enraged; I seemed to have hit the mark.

"It's not that *I* am incapable; the quest itself is clearly impossible!"

I couldn't help but be puzzled.

"Impossible?"

"My attacks have no effect, and no matter how many golems I materialize, I cannot advance a single step beyond the gatekeeper. The trial is being tampered with!"

Not sensing any dishonesty, I lowered my gaze toward the ground.

"...That's...not an exaggeration?"

"Certainly not! It's obvious that the Guardian Spirit has issued a quest that is impossible for everyone except you!"

I raised my gaze to meet Phillip's; I needed to know what he really wanted.

"…And what do you expect me to do? Need I remind you that I *lost* to you?"

Clearly emphasizing that word, I turned away again.

"It's simple: enter the labyrinth and retrieve that object. I'm sure the gatekeeper won't attack you or even appear at all. After all, you're *his* favorite."

"And if you're wrong?"

He smirked.

"Then die."

I glared at him in response to those absurd options, but he wasn't intimidated in the least.

"You do remember who I have here, *right?*"

He pointed at the golem who was holding my sister hostage, a victorious smirk on his face. There was no need to worry, though.

I dropped the act.

"What do you make of this, my dear Guardian Spirit?"

Out of nowhere, that brown lizard that Phillip and I both loathed materialized next to me. Phillip's smirk transformed into an expression of pure terror.

"Since…when…?"

"From the beginning, I'd say?"

At the nonchalance with which I delivered my reply, Phillip looked mortified.

"Your invisibility spell must be quite useful in situations like this."

"And yet you always seem to find me immediately."

Yes, immediately…not that it was by choice—I had simply happened to notice the Guardian Spirit while rushing to the cave and, as insurance, asked him to covertly follow me.

"So…mind telling us what kind of difficulty level you set that guardian to? To remain unscathed after an all-out assault by someone like Phillip is absurd!"

"I…was also surprised to hear that."

"Huh?"

I was speechless.

"It is true that the gatekeeper is difficult to get past, but I did not order it to be *that* ruthless."

What is that supposed to mean?

"…You agree that this is an emergency and you'll tell it to back off while I retrieve that object, right?"

I didn't know what expression the Guardian Spirit was making, since I was not very familiar with lizards, but I was sure that he was in deep thought.

"…Understood. However, I will invalidate the trial as well."

"No—it's still on."

I may not have been too familiar with lizards, but even I could tell that he was indignant.

"No matter how unsportsmanlike Phillip is being, the trial is still valid—you didn't specify any additional rules."

"But…"

"Besides, you owe me a favor, *right?*"

Domizio had no choice but to remain silent when faced with my threat.

"…All right…"

After obtaining his approval, I repeated Domizio's decision to Phillip so that he wouldn't misunderstand.

"Hear that? So let my sister go now."

"…Are you kidding me?!"

Phillip resumed a hostile attitude.

"How can I be sure that you're not plotting together? Or that you won't keep that object for yourself in the end?"

This is bad.

Domizio and I weren't collaborating, but the fact that he was with me was suspicious, and I couldn't prove anything. In the end, there was nothing that I could do.

"Bring me that object and I won't do anything to your sister."

I clenched my fists at my powerlessness.

"…All right."

I headed for the stairs that led to the labyrinth, but Domizio appeared suddenly and stopped me in my tracks.

"Take this with you."

He tossed me a lizard-shaped brooch.

"It's a special communication device. It will allow you to talk to me no matter the distance, although it won't work if there is too much magical noise in the area. I will guide—"

"No need."

I threw the brooch back at its owner.

"Phillip no doubt left some marks to find his way; that's all I'll need."

With that, I tried to continue forward, but I fell flat on my face instead.

"What are you doing?!"

As I tried to stand up, I turned and shouted at the lizard who had knocked me down, but Domizio had already moved from that spot: he had somehow climbed on top of my uniform shirt. His lightness for his size caught me off guard.

After I finally managed to shake him off, I saw that the brooch was firmly attached to the left side of my collar.

"Call it an abundance of caution."

I walked off, not saying anything at first. After a short while, I murmured to myself:

"That meddling lizard…"

I wasn't exactly complaining about his concern, though.

At last, no obstacles remained before me.

I headed into the bleak darkness of the crevasse. Turning my attention away from how deep it might be, I noticed that the steps were carved unnaturally. It was most likely the work of the Guardian Spirit; the path was well lit from its edge by luminescent plants, so that nobody would accidentally fall into the void.

I descended the first few steps. The temperature dropped dramatically.

I continued, paying close attention to where I placed my feet; I wondered why Domizio hadn't at least erected some guard rails. By the time I reached the end of the staircase about fifteen minutes later, the temperature had decreased even further. It wasn't so cold that it hindered my movements, but it would certainly be an issue if I stayed for too long.

The dim light from the luminescent plants—now far sparser than before—revealed an opening in the mossy wall, which was formed from rocks of various sizes. Placing a hand on the vegetation, I noticed no signs of any care.

The Guardian Spirit isn't the type to do periodic maintenance, huh.

I turned to see the rock wall out of which the stairs that I had just walked down had been hewn. Looking up, I could just barely make out the faint glow of the floor where my sister was waiting for me.

Suddenly, a dull ache pierced my chest.

"…"

Shapeless words escaped my lips. I shook my head to dispel that uncomfortable feeling. Deciding to stop my curiosity there, I headed into the cold, dark labyrinth.

"Guardian Spirit, how long will it take for me to reach the goal?"

"Perhaps an hour."

Domizio's voice could be heard loud and clear from the brooch.

An hour, huh...?

Mentally preparing myself for a lengthy journey, I walked down the corridor, finally reaching the first fork in the road. As a result of the poor lighting, it took me a few seconds to adjust to my surroundings.

My body shivered from the frigid air...and what I saw made my blood run cold.

"What the...?"

"Is something the matter?"

Domizio's voice wasn't the least bit surprised; if anything, he seemed puzzled by my reaction.

What's going on?

A terrifying number of animal corpses littered the path, their blood and entrails smeared across the wall in the shape of an arrow—probably Phillip's doing.

"...Nothing."

Without my realizing it, my voice became hoarser. Gritting my teeth, I mentally prepared myself.

Just as I had anticipated, the ghastly scene repeated itself at the next crossroads. And the next. Bats, snakes, mice...the corpses were as varied as they were numerous. The only difference between scenes was the size of the sanguine arrow.

I trudged forth with heavy steps, my emotions getting the better of me.

Was this slaughter really necessary?!

Such animals were practically helpless before Phillip's might.

Was this really the only fate awaiting the strong? To bathe in the blood and viscera of one's enemies on a ceaseless march into the unknown?

Is there really...no other path in front of me?

Deep in my thoughts, I belatedly noticed a strong source of magic appearing right behind me. I turned around and saw the figure of a bipedal reptile, its scales glowing in the dark. I would never have realized that it was a summoned creature if it weren't for the fact that its magical structure was completely different from a living being. With its sharp claws and menacing maw, it had several options to rend me limb from limb, but it... didn't.

"Domizio, what are you doing?"

"..."

The only response I received was the commencement of the creature's assault. Drawing my catalyst from its sheath, I managed to intercept the attack. Although my weapon had a slender form, it managed to bear the brunt of the summon's charge, holding it in place.

Material catalysts were developed from magic wands; however, they did not share the same weakness as their predecessors. Formed from an alloy of aluminum and a magical mineral called chrystiolite, they allowed for magical conduction on par with magic wands while maintaining a resistance to physical attack that far surpassed conventional weapons.

After deflecting the creature's claws and narrowly avoiding a kick, I realized that it was covertly gathering magical power within its mouth.

Hey... You can't be serious!

Anticipating the clichéd attack, I distanced myself from my opponent and dived to the ground, dodging the magic beam and rolling into a more favorable position. With our positions now reversed, I hurried to regain my balance before the next attack, but I noticed that my opponent had stopped moving. It took me a few seconds to realize the creature's goal.

If I wanted to continue toward the goal, I would have to fight the summon. By cutting off the option to proceed without confrontation, Domizio was leaving me no choice but to fight. Retreat was not an option—there was no way I could abandon my sister. It was my responsibility as her brother, and...

My emotions now unstable, I could no longer hide my frustration.

"So you're determined to get in my way...?"

I stepped forward. Unexpectedly, the creature in front of me took a step backward...but my mind did not register that action.

Slowly, my legs carried me further and further forward until I overtook the obstacle that had stood between me and my destination. After what seemed like an eternity without any further exchanging of blows, the creature disappeared into thin air.

"...I went too far. I'm sorry..."

In an almost inaudible voice, Domizio sought my forgiveness. It was difficult to reprimand him when he responded like this.

"...Don't do that again, okay?"

"..."

I received no response, but I was sure that it wouldn't happen again.

It was impossible for that creature to have escaped the control of the Guardian Spirit; Domizio had said that this cave was practically a part of himself. I highly doubted that he would fail to notice the movement of a single insect within the cave, let alone the actions of his own summons.

As I continued on my way, I noticed that the lighting was becoming dimmer and dimmer. Even though the luminescent plants still covered the walls, something unusual was happening… I stopped in my tracks to check my surroundings.

"…"

I thought so.

"Domizio."

"…Yes?"

His answer was delayed, as if he were zoning out. I was curious about what could distract a Guardian Spirit, but the current situation was more critical.

"Are there still many animals left in this cave?"

"Why do you ask?"

"Please just answer the question."

Understanding my urgency, Domizio remained silent for a few seconds.

"Not many. Until a few days ago, there were many more, but it seems like someone *eliminated them."*

"I see…"

"…What's the issue?"

I chose my words carefully before responding.

"…At this rate, the ecosystem in this cave will soon be no more."

"What is that supposed to mean?"

I approached one of the many faintly glowing flowers and unsheathed my catalyst, drawing a small magic circle in the air. As if reacting to my spell, the flower glowed brightly before fading completely. I couldn't help but be dissatisfied.

"The fates of flora and fauna are linked. With the decline of one, the other will soon follow."

"How can you be sure?"

"You know what type of plants cover the whole cave, right?"

Although I was pointing at the luminous greenery with my other hand, I realized that I was making a useless gesture—Domizio wasn't with me. That didn't mean that he couldn't understand what I was talking about, though.

"You mean these plants that generate light?"

"Do you know how they produce it?"

"…I know the basics of how to take care of a plant, but unfortunately, I've never been terribly interested in the field."

I sighed, but I couldn't blame him. Even though it was one of the most common plants inside caves, only botanists and scholars knew the details of this phenomenon.

"Unlike plants on the surface, these plants have no access to sunlight for photosynthesis. Instead, through a mutation, they are able to gain nourishment by absorbing magical power from surrounding living creatures. Additionally, after absorbing this magical power, these plants emit light."

I wasn't completely sure, but it didn't seem like the Guardian Spirit's magical power was able to nourish the plants in this labyrinth. Was it because he was too far away, or…?

"I see… What of it?"

Domizio asked for a conclusion, interrupting my train of thought.

"As the number of creatures in the cave decreases, so does the source of nourishment for these plants."

"Mother Nature is a tough mistress; I'm sure these plants will recover when new animals are born."

Domizio's statement made some sense. Time will heal all manner of wounds, even those caused by human hands.

"If the cave still exists…"

"What do you mean by that…?"

It seemed like Domizio was finally starting to understand.

"If nothing changes, the cave will collapse."

Domizio said nothing.

"Just as artificial caves need support beams to continue existing, natural caves will collapse without natural supports, and these plants have precisely this purpose in this ecosystem. Individually, they are not large, but their sheer number and the fact that they cover the entire cave combine to create a wide network of intersecting roots that holds the cave in place."

I was sure that Domizio was also contributing in some way to the structural support of this underground place, but how long could that last?

A year? A decade? And what about if one day Domizio were no longer present…?

"…It's just a theory, but I'm quite convinced of it."

"…And what would you like to do?"

I didn't know how to answer that; what *did* I want to do?

"…you will save…"

Suddenly, I remembered *her* words.

"At the moment, I can't do anything, but…"

I didn't complete the sentence, instead resuming on my path.

I can't do anything right now, but when this is over…

Without realizing it, I began to smile.

***

"…Am I there yet?"

While I was pondering this, the labyrinth's tunnel suddenly widened significantly, becoming comparable to the hall at the entrance of the cave. As I ascended the long staircase, the temperature slowly rose.

Here, too, countless luminescent plants were scattered, making the sight so bright that it took my eyes a few seconds to adjust to it. A majestic plant hung from the ceiling as if it were a chandelier. Coiling around a stalactite, it illuminated the entire room imposingly from above. The light reflected off some minerals; after a careful examination, I determined that they were chrystiolite.

While chrystiolite was commonly used by magicians, this did not mean that it was an abundant mineral. The presence of so much of the gemstone here made me suspicious of the true nature of the cave.

I looked around and saw a strange boulder that stood out on the opposite side of this perfectly leveled terrain. Although there was nothing of note on the right side of the hall, on the left side, there was a closed door identical to the one that Phillip had unsuccessfully tried to destroy several days earlier. The pair of doors were most likely linked.

"…"

I approached it and attempted to open it, but to no avail. I felt a mixture of relief and dejection when I saw the pointlessness of my actions.

My sister is just behind this door…

The thought that I had to go back all the way to the beginning was lowering my morale.

"Simon, what are you doing?"

I heard Domizio's voice from the brooch on my shirt collar.

"Nothing important. Where is the item that I'm supposed to retrieve?"

"It should be resting atop the pedestal opposite from the entrance. Can you see it?"

I stared at the strange boulder that had immediately caught my attention. Walking toward it, I couldn't notice anything out of the ordinary.

It was at that moment that I remembered Phillip's words:

"My attacks have no effect, and no matter how many golems I materialize, I cannot advance a single step beyond the gatekeeper. The trial is being tampered with!"

There was no sign of the infamous gatekeeper.

My premonition became reality when a tremor stopped me in my tracks. I tried to keep my balance, but the shuddering was growing in intensity.

"Impossible!"

At that moment, I did not comprehend Domizio's words, but when I saw the ground in front of me rising and forming a specific shape, I understood.

An enormous dragon was blocking my way.

Its height could not have exceeded five meters, but it *more* than made up for it with length. Arranged sideways, it filled half the width of the room. Pitch-black claws that absorbed all light from the surrounding plants, lustrous ridges that glowed eerily in the dark, and vacant eyes that seemed like they would not care if the entire world crumbled into dust around it—this was the creature that stood before me.

"...Hey, didn't you say that you'd keep your creatures at bay?!"

Protesting with every last drop of air in my lungs, I tried to pull back as far as I could and keep my balance while the earth shuddered.

"It's not a simple creature; I can't control it!"

With but a single roar from the dragon, stalactites fell to the ground like a fusillade of arrows. I dodged the spike that was about to impale me by a hair's breadth, only to find myself in the dragon's line of sight...

Observing it carefully, I saw a certain resemblance to Domizio.

That's why he said it wasn't a simple creature!

With a simple swipe of its forelimb, the dragon summoned an indomitable wave of air pressure that threw me about ten meters backward. Hurriedly bracing for impact, I managed to get away with just a few scratches. The creature eagerly attempted to approach me, but solid chains materialized on its four legs.

"Hey, are you all right?"

"Does it look like it?! Do something!"

"I'm trying, but it doesn't listen to my orders!"

"Didn't you say it was your alter ego?!"

Using all of my remaining energy to rebuke him, I seemed to have stunned Domizio.

"…Could it be…?"

"Do you have any idea what the problem might—"

Before I could finish my question, the imprisoned creature began to manipulate the airflow as if it were part of its body; it created a powerful gust of wind that rushed toward its mouth.

Aren't you a bit too comfortable with that move?!

"…! Run for it, Sim—"

Domizio's voice was drowned out—not by the whistling of the wind but by the magical noise the dragon created—but I knew what he meant; I directed my energy into my legs and threw myself to the side with all my might.

The next second, an intense magic bullet barely missed me. Simply being grazed by that attack threw me into the air like I weighed nothing at all.

I collided with one of the cave walls. My body was still intact…but the wall wasn't so lucky. An impressive crater was all that was left of the wall that had previously been behind me, and the ceiling had partly collapsed, blocking my only escape route. Regardless, that attack didn't seem to threaten the cave's existence.

I couldn't help but admire the sturdiness of this *prison*. Even my body hadn't sunk into the wall at all; it had rejected the entire impact.

Collapsed on the ground, I didn't seem capable of moving anymore. Blood clouded my vision and my entire body was numb; I couldn't even tell how injured I was.

And yet I stood up.

My muscles screamed with pain. My legs, chest, arms, and even head all felt as if they were on fire. I was sure that I had innumerable broken bones. The taste of blood was intense as it overflowed from my mouth.

My whole body was in agony. So why did I still stand?

I watched the dragon roar from in front of me. An aura of immense sadness and loss emanated from its awe-inspiring form.

"KRRRH…"

…Why…?

Somehow, I felt like my heart could understand its voice.

"GROOOOOOOOOOOOARGH!"

WHY COULDN'T I SAVE HIM?!

A plaintive cry that tore at my heartstrings.

At that moment, its eyes met mine. With another roar, it began to prepare another one of its magic bullets.

"Huh…"

Is it finally my time…to leave this cruel world?

This reality surely didn't need me.

However—

"…You must not die…"

Her voice echoed louder than ever inside my soul. My heart overflowed with determination.

"No matter how sad you may be…I must not die!"

That's right—I had to return to *her* side.

Because I'm…

- Another point of view -

The ground shook.

The walls shook.

The ceiling shook.

And with each tremor, boulders fell. I raised a barrier to ensure that no one would be hurt under my watch.

For the past ten minutes, explosions had been ringing out incessantly from the other side of the cave. Phillip and I were both anxious about these quakes that seemed like they would never end. Even though I was connected to this cave and should therefore understand everything that happened inside of it, I was unable to determine the cause of this unceasing barrage. And that wasn't all—I couldn't even control that creature...

Yes, my alter ego was the cause of this catastrophe.

As much as I wanted to rush to Simon's side, I still had to go through the labyrinth, and it would take me at least half an hour no matter how quickly I ran. The only other path was *that* door, but it was no use; without approval from the Guardian Spirit of Earth, that is, *me*, that door would remain firmly shut. Only one whom I deemed from the depths of my soul to be worthy of being my companion could open that door, and it was not a rational decision.

Even though it was an emergency, I was powerless to help.

Just like that time...

In the end, all I could do was wait. And, as if I had willed it, the explosions eventually ceased. A restless silence suffused the room. Grasping this opportunity, I tried to re-establish direct communication with the student who was in danger:

"Simon! Are you there? What's the situation?"

But there was no response. All I could hear was the buzz of magical interference.

"What happened? H-hey, answer me!"

That troublesome student had evidently recovered from shock and asked me a reasonable question. I would have answered him...if he hadn't taken a person hostage.

The only person who was truly oblivious to the situation was that precious sister of the student I wished to become my representative.

No.

It was more accurate to say that Simon reminded me of my only companion.

"So you're determined to get in my way...?"

Had I really learned nothing? Would I once again hide from the truth before me and leave it all to fate? I—

As if my wish had been heard, a door opened.

No, I had not been dreaming; that door, which I had long considered inaccessible, had just been opened by a student who was covered in fresh blood and grit. Simon Anion breathed in heaving gasps, unable to hide his exhaustion.

Did he manage to beat my alter ego?

I couldn't believe in that possibility. My alter ego was not a pitiful being like my current form and possessed far more magical power than a mere student could ever hope to oppose. Yet the student in front of me...

With uncertain steps, he slowly approached us. Terrified, Phillip began retreating furiously...but since the golem he had summoned was behind him, his retreat was short-lived.

That student threw something toward the troublesome one, who caught it in midair, clearly dismayed.

"Here. Now give me my sister back."

Although he was bleeding profusely in several places, Simon Anion seemed more concerned about his sister's health than his own.

"A...watch...?"

In Phillip's hands was a pocket watch forged of pure silver. Its metal cover featured the golden outline of a butterfly and was adorned with five precious gems, each representing one of the main magical elements.

That same outline was depicted inside the quadrant where the intricately ornamented hands should have moved. Yes, *should* have moved. While one might think it a malfunction, this was its original state—from the beginning, this timepiece was incomplete.

Suddenly, Phillip laughed.

"...I understand. All those earthquakes... That door... They're part of an act that the two of you planned, aren't they?"

Looking at both Simon and me, he didn't even trust the wounds that covered *that* student's entire body.

"Is this the item that you requested?"

Seeking confirmation, Phillip showed me the watch.

"...Yes."

"So now I'm the Earth representative, correct?"

I didn't say anything.

How stupid can one be?!

Obsessed with victory, he had lost sight of everything else.

"…He's now the Earth representative…right?"

Simon asked me the same question with a somewhat threatening glance. I presumed that he wished to get this over with as soon as possible…

But I couldn't allow it.

"I will never accept someone like you as my representative."

Both Phillip's and Simon's expressions contorted with anger.

"Why?!"

For Phillip, that question was so natural; he seemed even more clueless than I had anticipated. Thus, I started from the beginning:

"Firstly, you lost the duel against Simon."

Phillip's expression turned into one of bewilderment, while Simon's became one that screamed 'Now you say so?!'

The two fell silent.

"Do you truly believe that I would not notice you transferring magical power to your golem at the moment of the explosion, hardening its armor just enough to withstand the impact? That you could trick *my* eyes with just that?"

"Then why did you proclaim me the winner?"

"It's simple: I wanted to see Simon's determination."

Phillip didn't want to believe those words.

"If the outcome of the duel had been clear, I would have been unable to do anything about it, but I took advantage of that situation to get what I wanted. In short, *two can play at that game.*"

Phillip covered his ears like a frightened child.

"That…that's not true!"

"That is why you were not even qualified to begin this trial. And I have not even begun to discuss the methods you used to obtain your 'victory.'

"Phillip Royals, you are unworthy of being the representative of my element."

"SHUT UP!"

A cry that contained all of his pent-up emotions echoed through the cavern. That unworthy boy clenched his fists intensely in frustration, causing his nails to pierce the skin of his palms. Blood began to flow, staining even the watch that he had just received.

"I am the only one who can become Earth representative! After swallowing my pride and putting up with that…that *fool* of a former representative, I finally managed to get into his good graces and become his nominee for representative. I will gain the power to become the strongest and obtain what I have long sought!"

He had gone mad—that was the only impression he was giving.

"…You."

He glared at Simon, who was a few meters in front of him.

"If only you had never enrolled at the academy…"

But instead of moving forward, he began backing away…

"Now take your love for your sister…"

…backing away to the edge of the precipice—

"Stop!"

***

Time stood still.

Phillip—did not heed my warning and was reaching toward Marie.

Marie—was suspended in midair, supported only by Phillip's golem.

Simon—was running toward his sister at breakneck speed.

One step—that is the distance that separates them. A distance that is so close and yet so far. The same as on that day.

Time resumed its inexorable march.

He's not going to make it.

✱✱✱

"…and follow her into the next life!"

Phillip flung Marie off the precipice, a vainglorious smirk on his face.

With not a hint of hesitation, Simon threw himself into the abyss, snapping me out of my inner thoughts.

"What are you doing?!"

There was no response.

I rushed as close to the edge as I could, but all I could see was the siblings embracing each other as the infinite void welcomed them into *its* embrace.

All I could hear was Phillip's mad laughter echoing through the air.

"Now that he's gone, I'm the only possible candidate! Isn't that right, AHAHAHAHA!"

All traces of humanity had long since left this disgusting…*thing*.

Something tore at my chest.

No, it was not physical pain. I felt as if something *else* were being pierced and torn; something was happening to the cave!

Just as I came to this conclusion, a deafening noise thundered from the depths of the abyss.

It soon faded into silence, but Phillip's look of shock and dread remained. Trying to deny the possibility, he backed away fearfully.

In my heart, I was hoping that it was not a dream, and—

A tremendous surge of magical power the likes of which I had not felt in centuries exploded out of the abyss, and two students appeared from within. In this silent world, their bodies screamed out of the darkness before gently landing atop the edge of the precipice as if unfettered by the laws of gravity.

Hugging Marie tightly in his arms, Simon spoke in my direction.

"…Why not?"

I did not know what he was referring to, but I could sense him seething.

"Why is it that you do not appoint him as your representative and give him the power he longs for?"

At those words, both Phillip and I were speechless. Appointed academic representatives received a great font of magical power from their Guardian Spirit so that they would be able to easily resolve academic disputes, play an important role in the kingdom's political discussions, and even command an army in the unlikely event of war.

This was no small power: it would turn even an ordinary citizen into a war machine capable of destroying an entire city.

"I will knock him off the pedestal that he's so proud of—"

Simon's next words were addressed to me.

"—and show you the *true determination* that you seek!"

Chills ran all over my body. *I was beginning to regret ever having provoked him.*

012: The Truth

"Are you sure?"

I wanted to ascertain Simon's true intentions…

"…"

…but all I got was an emotionless look. He probably didn't want to repeat himself. After gathering my resolve, I walked up to the other…student.

"Are you prepared to receive the power of an academic representative?"

Stunned, Phillip seemed not to understand what was occurring. It took him a few seconds to realize that the situation he had longed for was coming true. A look of elation took root in his face.

"…Excellent! It seems you understand who the *true* academic representative is, after all."

Having received Phillip's consent, I decided as to…how large of a rampage I would allow him to go on.

If the worst comes to the worst, I will forcibly cut the flow of magic.

Convincing myself with this flimsy excuse, I started the appointment ceremony. A dark brown glow the color of the finest loam enveloped Phillip's entire body. Using the pocket watch as a medium, I linked our magic circuits.

"!!!"

His expression warped into a bigger and bigger grin.

"My power has grown two-…no, fivefold! It's…incredible!"

Actually, I increased it twenty*fold…*

Evidently, the limit of his control was about five times his normal amount. Despite my quip, however, I could not deny that a prodigy stood before me. Since magicians were sensitive to magical power, entering an environment densely occupied by magic particles or attempting to control a significantly larger amount of magical power than usual often caused discomfort that took time to adjust to. However, Phillip showed no signs of this and was visibly improving his control over his newfound power.

"Domizio…"

I heard Simon's voice clearly in my mind. I turned toward him and found that he was using the brooch that I had given him. While Phillip was training to master his new magical reserves, I approached Simon timidly…but his expression had changed.

He looked…*kind.*

"I have a favor to ask of you."

He placed Marie on the ground with extraordinary care.

"Could you please look after her?"

The contrast between his current demeanor and that of just a few minutes ago was so stark that it took me several seconds to process his words. I nodded.

"Thank you, truly."

He started striding confidently toward Phillip, but I interrupted him with a question:

"Are you sure you can beat him?"

"He who dares harm my sister condemns himself to a lifetime of suffering!"

His tone was so boundlessly confident that he sounded like a completely different person.

Stopping perhaps twenty meters away from his opponent, Simon waited for Phillip to finish his preparations. Perhaps Phillip was too drunk with power to notice, but the distance between the two of them was the same as in their previous duel.

But will Simon fight seriously this time?

***

"Pardon the wait."

It took only a few minutes for Phillip to ready himself. I was honestly impressed by his speed of adjustment; an average representative would have taken several days at a minimum just to endure the intensity of the magical flow.

If only he had a better attitude, maybe...

No. I could no longer deny it: although more exceptional people could very well exist, it was the student opposite from Phillip that had me rapt.

"No excuses, now. Is that right?"

"...What do you mean?"

"For when I shatter your delusions of grandeur and show you the truth that you've been hiding from!"

I was surprised by Simon's taunt, and I wasn't the only one. Fighting spirit radiated from Phillip's every pore; he was clearly furious.

"You'll regret challenging me!"

Simon did not respond immediately.

A beat later—

"Not before I make you regret harming my sister."

It was at that moment that two enormous magical auras expanded like an explosion, filling the room.

Phillip's amount of magical power was obvious, since he was gathering power directly from my source, but what was the source of Simon's power? Had he been hiding it from the beginning? At that moment, I felt a familiar chill down my spine.

It was terror. And regret.

Huh?

I didn't know why, but the power overflowing from Simon was somehow nostalgic. I started doubting myself.

But he...died!

This could mean only one thing—Simon's existence must be similar to *his*.

An Earth golem rose from the ground that separated the two students. As in the previous duel, it took the shape of a knight equipped with a shield on its left and a weapon on its right, but unlike before, its weapon was a spear...and it stood twenty meters high. Despite the golem's immense size, this expansive hall's ceiling was over twice as tall; even a colossus like this could move about with ease.

"...Unbelievable! So I acquired this much power...!"

Phillip, astonished by and drunk with his newfound power, was molding his golem in more detail than before. Simon, meanwhile, was standing still, watching the scene impassively.

"Is that all?"

Thus provoked, Phillip paused his sculpting.

"Let's see if you're still in the mood to boast after *this!*"

In complete defiance of its physical size, the golem launched an attack with its weapon in the direction of Simon, who didn't seem to react.

"What are you doing?! Dodge it!"

Fearing the worst, I decided to forcibly cut the flow of magic—but a hand stopped me.

"No need."

The physical contact distracted me, and the spear mercilessly struck the ground. A cloud of sand rose, obscuring Simon's figure. He didn't dodge in any direction, and nor was he thrown by the impact. To make matters worse, the spear was clearly embedded deep in the ground.

As much as I might have wanted Simon to block the spear with his body, it was simply impossible for a mere human to withstand a direct hit from a twenty-meter golem.

He is most likely...

"Bahahaha! This time, it didn't even take two moves!"

Phillip ordered the golem to retract its spear, aiming to reveal Simon's corpse...

...but what it revealed instead was the back of a certain boy as he casually dangled from the spear's shaft, holding onto a long monochrome sword that was wedged in it.

Where did he draw that sword from?!

Before Phillip could process this information, Simon swung himself onto the spear and bounded up it with incredible agility, bringing him face to face with the golem; only then did Phillip finally realize that this was not the swift victory that he had imagined.

Soon enough, the force of gravity took effect, and Simon started to fall. His face showed no sign of exertion or anxiety. On the contrary, *he looked completely at ease.*

He tossed the sword he was holding aside and drew a bizarre magic circle. The spell shattered, revealing a normal-sized sword hilt...attached to a blade that was more than five meters long!

Still falling, Simon pointed his sword at the golem knight's right shoulder and began cutting through it with seemingly no effort whatsoever. Soon, he had reached the golem's armpit, and not only had his fall not slowed in the slightest, Simon continued to accelerate.

With not a hint of emotion on his face, the boy soon positioned himself for landing.

This—was absurd. Falling from a height of twenty meters and hoping to remain unscathed was impossible, to say nothing of slicing through that stone arm as if it were made of dry leaves. But Simon did both without even breaking a sweat, creating a crater when he landed on his feet.

Leaping sideways at an impressive speed to avoid the falling arm, Simon sliced through the golem's left ankle as well. As if it had fulfilled its raison d'être, the weapon shattered into motes of magical energy, which dispersed into the environment.

With its balance utterly destroyed, the golem knight began to fall toward Simon, who then returned to his original position with a casual hop as if the fight had never begun. This effect was ruined by the conspicuous heap of rubble that lay between the impassive Simon and the incredulous Phillip, however.

""How...?""

Both Phillip and I were astounded. I couldn't hope to understand the depths of the student in front of me, and Phillip no doubt felt the same.

"I'll say it one more time: is that all?"

Phillip's incredulity morphed into fury as he once again gathered enough magical power to create an Earth golem, but...

"Hey, you've got to be kidding me..."

An even more titanic golem than before was currently being shaped. His previous golem had likely been summoned using approximately a quarter of his power; I estimated that he was now pushing his limits and using perhaps a third.

I was amazed that he was able to master this much of his newfound power during his first fight. His opponent, however, was unimpressed:

"If that's all you've got, I don't even need to change the spell."

And it was at that moment that I finally saw the inscription of Simon's magic circle.

Each spell required a specific code, which was inscribed inside the magic circle used. Normally, each catalyst could store a spell to speed up the process, but Simon wasn't even using one—although he created each magic circle from scratch, he completed them as fast as lightning!

I focused my gaze, bringing his code into view. I almost couldn't believe my eyes.

"Impossible..."

That code...was to summon an Earth golem!

How did he get a sword out of that spell?!

The moment I asked myself that, Simon extended his hand into the magic circle and destroyed it. This time, no weapons appeared. Instead, the magic particles scattered, but not in an illogical way: they swirled in a vortex around Simon's body, soon mantling him as if this were the natural order of things.

Before Phillip's golem had been fully completed, Simon sprang toward its right leg and threw a simple fist. It connected, throwing the golem to the ground to meet its predecessor.

The golem disintegrated before it had even fully materialized.

This time, Simon decided to stroll back to his original position as if he wanted to highlight the situation. Phillip fell to his knees.

"How... How is it possible...? Who...are you...?"

Simon's expression contorted for the first time in the fight. He clenched his fists tightly to calm himself, then declared the reason for Phillip's defeat:

"The golems you summon have a fatal weakness."

With those words, he had Phillip's entire attention.

"Ordinary Earth golems are lumps of magic that are then shaped, but yours are slightly different: you only place the magic on the surface to grant them greater sturdiness, but if even one crack appears, they are as fragile as glass!"

"Ordinary Earth golems are lumps of magic that are then shaped, but yours are slightly different: you only place the magic on the surface to grant them greater sturdiness, but if even one crack appears, they are as fragile as glass!"

Simon's reasoning was sound, but he had glossed over one crucial detail: *how much force is needed to form that crack?!*

Earth magic was fundamentally based on shaping magical power and hardening it so solidly that it could withstand much more powerful attacks than conventional weapons could. Considering that Phillip was using eight times his usual amount of magic, just how strong was Simon to defeat him without even having to catch his breath?

Faced with reality, Phillip was desperate. I couldn't be sure what he was thinking, but his face betrayed the fear that he was feeling. His own talent must have told him the gap between them, and he started to ramble:

"I get it now! You must have received power from the Guardian Spirit as well!"

He was wrong. Simon had won under his own power.

"Then I just have to use more of that lizard's power than you!"

As if answering Phillip's desire, the timepiece began to emit an intense glow, which soon completely enveloped him.

"It can't be!"

I tried to cut the flow of magic, but to no avail. Simon must have sensed the danger, for he bounded backward until he reached my side and asked me a question while keeping his eyes trained on Phillip:

"Hey, what's going on?!"

"He must have lost control; the magic source is taking over!"

We could do nothing but observe the scene. I prayed for the remote possibility that the phenomenon would stop by itself; interfering with such an enormous amount of out-of-control magic was tantamount to suicide. Forget Phillip—the resulting explosion would at the very least level the entire academy!

Fortunately, the glow began to fade, revealing another golem. It was smaller in stature than its predecessors at around fifteen meters tall, but the magic aura that it emitted was far more powerful.

There was not the slightest glimpse of Phillip's figure.

"Don't tell me that Phillip is..."

"He's inside that golem!"

I didn't doubt Simon's word; the worst-case scenario had already happened.

"He must have tried to control more magical power than he could handle, and as a result, my alter ego...!"

"Hey, what's that supposed to mean?!"

I hesitated to reveal the truth. If I shared this information, I might put Simon in a position from which there would be no return.

"Domizio."

It was as if he had read my mind. However, rather than berating me…

"Think of it as repaying the debt you owe me."

…he was giving me an excuse. Accepting it, I decided to tell him the truth:

"That watch has a direct link to my body. Phillip was not using simple magical power; within that watch lie my emotions."

Magical power is present in every creature of the world, but it only develops through emotions: the stronger the emotion, the more magical power one can summon. Thus, distraction brings poor results, and anger allows for more powerful—but uncontrollable—spells.

"Currently, I have a strong repressed desire: the desire to free myself."

Simon remained completely silent and still, not even blinking.

"…Don't you want to know why I want freedom?"

"I have no interest in the private life of a lizard."

At Simon's indifferent reply, I burst into a smile that I could not hide anymore. Despite the critical situation, I did not feel any tension. Simon gently broke me out of my reverie:

"So, about Phillip…?"

"…Ah, yes. At the moment, my alter ego is possessing the watch and using Phillip's body as a catalyst to manifest himself."

"So all I have to do is destroy that watch, and everything will go back to normal?"

I couldn't help but become depressed upon hearing Simon's incredibly basic, albeit sensible, plan.

"…It's not *quite* that simple."

I tried to look him in the eyes in a manner that would hint at the weight of what I was about to ask of him, but his gaze was still turned toward that golem. I faced it too.

"Simon Anion… Destroy that golem—together with Phillip."

Simon said nothing. I perceived neither disgust nor understanding; he seemed to be awaiting an explanation.

"…As time goes by, Phillip's body will be entirely consumed by the spell. Don't worry about him; defeat him before it is too late, and save the academy!"

I received no confirmation from Simon. It was at that moment that I had a suspicion.

Don't tell me he can't—

"Look, we're fighting underground! If this cave suffers too much damage, the whole academy will collapse!"

Phillip's life was just one; hundreds more innocents would be lost if the academy were leveled. I had to convince him to make the correct choice.

To kill Phillip.

At last, Simon responded:

"Then I just have to save him before that happens."

I couldn't believe my ears. Despite the situation and what Phillip had done to him, Simon had declared that he would save him.

"It's no use; you don't even know where the watch is! You could hit Phillip while trying to find it!"

Simon turned to me for the first time. It was at that moment that I finally realized what was strange about Simon's expression—no, about his eyes.

"Don't you remember? I can see what's inside that golem."

His pupils had dilated irregularly into a cross shape, and his irises now glowed a brilliant purple.

Those eyes...! They were...

Simon looked away and gazed at the girl behind me, who had remained silent throughout the entire discussion. Marie Anion's eyes were full of confidence.

"You can do it, Simon!"

Having obtained his sister's encouragement, Simon strode toward the golem.

"Why? Why are you pushing yourself so ha—"

"I'm human. That's why I'll save him!"

Human...?

His figure became smaller and smaller.

Don't joke with me; those are the eyes of a demon!

***

"…O mighty Guardian Spirit of Earth…?"

A voice politely requested my attention from behind me—it was a female Water student in her second year, with long chestnut hair and hazelnut eyes. Although she had been drugged, kidnapped, and almost killed, before becoming involved in a crazy fight, Marie Anion didn't seem worried in the least. Her expression was clear, without any trace of fear.

Becoming a bit shy because of her gaze and because I had endangered her safety (and also because being referred to with such formality was a bother to my ears), I spoke to her as an equal:

"Domizio is fine; you can drop the formalities."

"All right, Domizio, then. Well…"

Accepting my offer, Marie Anion spoke her mind:

"My brother is not a demon; he is human."

She had evidently sensed my doubt, but I quickly rebuked her:

"Human? Those eyes are proof that he's a demon!"

Irises that glowed a brilliant purple, pupils in the shape of a cross, eyes that could see magic itself… He was clearly a demon, but that wasn't even the most baffling thing; why did those eyes—the most distinctive trait of all demons—only show themselves now?!

Being clusters of emotions and magic, demons were irrational and usually had violent tendencies. The issues one would face when fighting a demon were numerous, but the worst of all was that they could not be destroyed.

No matter how much you stabbed, slashed, or pummeled, it was impossible to defeat a demon in honest combat. Magic was absolutely out of the question—the demon would only feed on it and become even stronger. Your only hope was to artificially accelerate the natural scattering of the demon's fragile emotions until it faded into nothingness, but that was difficult for even the most skilled of magicians.

Simon had none of these characteristics.

"Even though he has those eyes, Simon is human."

Marie's gaze showed no hesitation; her crystal-clear eyes did not fear the existence that she called her 'brother.'

"I am not like Simon… I don't have those eyes."

While I listened to Marie's explanation, Simon and the Earth golem were fighting untiringly. Simon's attacks were ineffectual because of the anti-magic properties of my alter ego; still, he summoned sword upon sword and continued his frenzied attack.

"Those eyes of his allow him to read the code of magic circles and extract only the necessary parts, transforming the rest into magical power that enhances his physical abilities."

Constantly darting from side to side to avoid the golem's attacks, Simon tried to devise a strategy to reach the timepiece, whose whereabouts were unknown.

"Wait a second… How does your brother have those eyes?"

Momentarily accepting the idea that Simon was human, I asked a fundamental question; a demon's eyes were exclusive to the race, and there was no documentation to the contrary. I myself could attest to this fact.

Marie's proud expression soon faded and was replaced by one of deep sadness. She bit her lips, seemingly recalling a painful memory.

"Because—we share no bond of blood…"

Of the many discoveries today, this was the least upsetting; it went without saying that she couldn't be the sister of a magical phenomenon.

"…but I am his sister!"

Yet she stubbornly repeated this statement as if it were fact, despite it having already been proven otherwise.

"This is one of the conditions that I imposed on him…"

"Imposed…?"

Failing to read the room, a magic bullet hit the barrier I had created at the start of the battle. Trying in vain to pierce my shield, it was repelled and embedded itself in the wall of this *prison.*

This underground space cannot withstand too many more impacts!

As if he had read my thoughts, Simon moved to intercept the bullets. Instead of focusing on offense, he targeted the numerous magic circles that appeared near him, making them disappear into thin air before I could even blink.

I couldn't believe my eyes.

"He erased all those spells in such a short time?!"

Despite this incredible feat, enough magic circles still remained to threaten the collapse of the cave. With no hesitation, Simon dashed toward the area with the highest density of spells, and with a double hand gesture, the magic circles closest to his body flipped over. As if they had changed masters, the spells were cast toward the golem.

"…Impossible! That ability—"

As if reading my mind, Marie completed my sentence:

"—is the same as that of the Demon King, Kinlarus. The ability to take the opponent's magic and wield it against its caster."

Kinlarus. The Demon King who was formerly my most trusted companion.

Memories that I had long sealed up arose. Tears of nostalgia poured from my eyes; *that's* why I had taken such an interest in Simon!

He reminded me of Laro in every aspect.

The only person who could control the demons in the war of two centuries past.

The person who went on to become the Demon King, Kinlarus.

"But how is that possible…?"

I watched Simon's figure, rapt. Jumping from one side of the golem's body to the other, he interrupted all of the magic circles it conjured one by one. Between its own spells being sent right back at it and the sheer number of swords that Simon kept throwing, my alter ego could not even gather enough power to produce projectiles capable of destroying the cave.

"Because he is a lineal descendant of Kinlarus. It's been quite a few generations, though."

Marie's explanation made no sense.

"There's no way Kinlarus had any heirs!"

"Why are you so sure?"

"Because…!"

Shocked, I did not know how to answer. Why *was* I so sure that he had no heirs?

Because he cast aside his humanity to become a demon?

Because of the irrationality inherent in all demons?

Because he betrayed me all those years ago?

Or because…I couldn't see him with anyone else but *her*?

"Whatever your beliefs may be, reality remains unchanged: Simon is a descendant of Kinlarus. However, because he also has human blood, he's not a true demon."

"How…"

Everything Marie had just said made complete sense. And yet, there was one thing that I could not hope to comprehend: how could she say all that in such a calm tone?

Never taking her eyes off her brother, Marie made a confession:

"At first, I was afraid."

Her pure eyes clouded over, now filled with tears.

"I was…afraid of Simon. When I first witnessed his powers, I didn't know what to do. I wanted to stay as far away from him as possible."

Simon stood atop the golem's head. Armed with another monochrome sword, he rushed down to stab it in the neck. The attack connected, but it wasn't enough to fully destroy the armor. The golem fought back, sweeping Simon away.

His figure crashed against the ground, stopping a few meters from the crevasse. Stabbing a new sword into the ground, he managed to avoid a second fall into the abyss, but, stunned by the blow, he struggled to regain his footing.

"And yet he never left me."

Slowly but surely, Simon stood up once more.

"No matter how much I pushed him away, he just kept on standing by my side."

With a look full of determination, Simon stared at the sword he had stuck in his opponent's neck.

"No matter how much I scolded him, he kept on smiling at me."

More and more blood ran down his face.

"As much as I hated him, he still loved me."

Even so, he sprang toward the golem so fast that he began to blur.

"And even with his own life at stake, he thought only of protecting me."

By continuing to erase and reverse the golem's spells, he began to make headway again.

"So I made up my mind—"

Summoning another sword, he stabbed it into the same position as before, but to no avail.

"—I decided to kill the demon inside him."

Simon was flung to the ground again.

"That's why I imposed three rules on him."

But he did not fall.

"Three rules to make him stop hating himself."

At a hesitant pace and with labored breathing, the demon—no, the boy—was still trying his best to move forward.

"Three rules to make him start loving himself."

A punch from the golem threatened to crush him—

"The first..."

—but he deflected it with yet another sword.

"...'I'm your sister, and it's all right to depend on me!'"

The boy leaped into the air.

"The second..."

The golem's other hand threatened to grab him—

"...'You must not die, because I need you!'"

—but it was sliced through by the weapon he was clenching and became a springboard for Simon to jump even faster.

"And the third..."

Simon summoned one last sword, this time much longer than before.

"...'Promise me that you will save anyone whom you see in danger before you...'"

Taking a deep breath, he tensed every single muscle in his body—

"*Because you are human.*"

—and thrust the sword deep into the golem's neck.

***

With the sound of the timepiece being shattered, the golem was enveloped in a blinding light and slowly faded into motes of magical energy. Phillip's body began to fall to the ground, but Simon grabbed him gently by the collar of his shirt and slung him over his shoulder.

He had kept his promise.

The boy slowly returned to earth, where his sister was patiently waiting for him.

"*This* is my brother!"

013: The Birth of a Lie

It was more than two centuries ago—an event that I will never forget.

The bloody, bitter war fought between the kingdoms of Gilar and Minnesa. In that conflict, all participants lost something.

And we, the Guardian Spirits of Gilar, lost everything.

Power, freedom, and even…our most trusted comrade. We all wondered, *How could this happen…?*

But we already knew the answer—it was a hollow question, solely intended as a form of self-flagellation.

It was thus that we accepted our retribution.

*****

It all began with an attempt by Minnesa to expand their territory. It was inevitable that sooner or later, they would have borne arms against us as their population grew; Minnesa was located on hostile, arid land and had no worthwhile exports.

However, contrary to what one might expect of a kingdom located in such a harsh environment, their technological and magical development had always been among the best on the continent. For this reason, in the first years of bitter conflict, Gilar suffered severe defeats.

Everything changed when two people arrived: a radiant young woman named Fina and a listless young man named Laro. No one could have expected these two to reverse the momentum of Gilar's army, but they did. The girl made use of three different catalysts to perform awe-inspiring spells of multiple elements, while the man was an anomaly who could subjugate demons with a practiced ease before wielding them against his enemies.

These two people, bound by blood, decided of their own volition to fight for the kingdom in which they lived. Achieving exceptional results, they were soon deployed to the main battlefront where we Guardian Spirits were fighting.

At first glance, the pair did not seem remarkable in any way: an ordinary, lively young woman and an ordinary, quiet young man. However, when they were on the battlefield, their skill was remarkable. Therefore, one question was inevitable:

"Why do you fight?"

The young woman answered simply:

"Because I love this country."

The radiance that her response exuded was unnatural in an era scarred by war.

When I turned my gaze to the young man instead, his response was dry:

"Because I care about my sister."

A rather mysterious answer.

"You're probably wondering why he lets me fight even though he wants to protect me, right?"

Correct.

"Because I'm sure my big brother can protect me from everything."

When the young woman answered, the young man's hand landed on her head, patting her as if he wished to reaffirm the warmth that he wanted to defend.

"If she wants to fight for this country, then I will help her. I won't let her die."

His gentle yet determined expression made me reflect on one thing for the first time ever:

What am I fighting for?

Slowly but surely, even the other Guardian Spirits became attached to this strange pair, and we fought side by side on the battlefield time after time.

Until finally, *that* day came. After repelling countless enemy offensives, we had finally arrived near their capital. If we had conquered that city, the war would have ended. Unfortunately, fate had other plans…

It was an overcast day, and the sounds of battle could scarcely be heard over the howling of the wind. Countless battles were fought; countless lives were lost. Man or woman, elder or youth—the specter of death did not discriminate. This area, a forest clearing perhaps five kilometers from the walls of Minnesa's capital, was no different.

There, those two precious siblings fought as if possessed, a veritable storm that would permit escape to none who sought to sully the country they so cherished. The sister engaged the human defenders, wielding tremendous multi-element magic to carve huge swathes into the enemy formation; the brother engaged any demons who were formed during the bloodshed, using previously unheard-of magic to unravel the pure malice and despair that formed their very beings and bend them to his will. Together, they were like twin stars in the night sky, a shining glimmer of hope that would bring a swift end this bloody war.

But this time was different; an ominous magic bullet approached the back of that taciturn youth, who was caught in particularly intense combat.

He's not going to notice!

"Laro!"

In a demonstration of the quick-wittedness for which he was known, he raised numerous magical barriers, each of them imbued with the body of a demon that he had previously subjugated.

I sighed with relief.

His barriers shattered instantly.

It took only a second for the light of one of those stars to be extinguished and the other to forever be tainted by darkness. The girl flung herself in front of her brother, protecting him with her beating heart.

The battlefield was dyed a familiar color.

She did not even have the chance to say her final words. As her brother held what was left of her with tears in his eyes, Fina's eyes lost all vitality. And yet, her expression was a peaceful one.

"Why are you…smiling?"

Laro's brown eyes, which had once shone so brightly, suddenly dimmed. A dark aura mantled him as his face contorted with loss—and rage.

Surrounded by innumerable magic circles, the young man summoned demon after demon that I had never seen before to his side. Those that he usually commanded were a weakened form of the originals, but *these* were truly sinister.

"DESTROY EVERYTHING!!!!!!"

And everything they did destroy.

With this command, the demons attacked the city and practically razed it to the ground. Only when the enemy raised a white flag did Laro come to his senses and collapse where he stood.

A few days later, after an armistice between the two nations had been signed, we Guardian Spirits arranged a funeral for Fina and buried her near her favorite lake. Laro visited her grave every day, his eyes filled with emotion.

Not despair—rage.

It was no wonder, for the bullet that had sought Laro's life was rather peculiar. After all, no matter how many attacks they had launched at him in previous battles, no one had ever even managed to scratch him.

Besides, the direction it had come from was strange too: it was as if the enemy had outflanked our forces in a split second. With the cooperation of my comrades, I began investigating independently of Laro.

As much as we wanted to help him directly, he continued to refuse our assistance, saying that it did not concern us. After I heard his explanation, something began cracking inside me.

Are we really strangers to you...?

Months passed, and we had still yet to discover the identity of the elusive spellcaster. And it was then that we received news of a fact that we had thought impossible.

"Laro...is attacking Gilar's forces?!"

Unable to believe my ears, I rushed to the new battlefield...the capital of Minnesa.

By the time I arrived, all of Gilar's soldiers had already been driven out of the city, and an immense number of demons were protecting it. And among the figures who stood on the walls of the castle, I saw *him*.

His appearance had undergone a tremendous transformation. Pale-faced and terribly fatigued, Laro commanded his summoned creatures. The aura surrounding him—which would make all but the bravest of heart shiver in its presence—expanded for just an instant; he had noticed my arrival. I could not see the expression in his purple eyes, but one thing was sure.

He was serious.

More than half a year of further conflict passed, and Laro's demonic army slowly encroached upon Gilar's territory. As he continued to receive reinforcements from Minnesa's army, which had scattered because of the armistice, the war only became more intense.

One night, I was apprised of a particular piece of intelligence:

"It seems that a few days ago, Laro disappeared, and the enemy army is in a state of total confusion."

Shrinking my body to a more human size—although my appearance was still reptilian and anyone could see the wings spreading from my shoulders—I raced to the only place that I could think of. There, I saw a familiar figure.

"As I imagined, you are here."

In front of his sister's grave, Laro prayed in silence. The only source of light was the torch that I had brought to politely signal my presence.

"It has been a year since her death, hasn't it?"

Fearlessly, I approached him.

"Laro… Tell me, why did you start this war?"

Unmoving, he continued to remain silent.

"Didn't your sister love this country?"

It was at that moment that Laro turned to face me. I was horrified by the drastic change that had taken place during the year we were separated.

His body was so pale that I doubted he was still human. To neglect the well-being of his body in this manner… It was a wonder that he could even stand upright. The only hint of energy that remained was his expression, smoldering with repressed anger.

"You know nothing about my sister!"

With tears in his eyes, his gaze carefully met mine.

"Why did the country she loved so much kill her?!"

I couldn't believe what he was saying. Seeing my reaction, Laro calmed down for a moment.

"So you don't know, huh…"

"What's that supposed to mean?!"

Trying to calm his inner turmoil, he looked up at the starry sky.

"…That bullet was a special spell cast by Gilar. It was meant only to kill me, and the people of Minnesa had nothing to do with it."

I couldn't believe it.

"Why… Why would they do that? You and your sister were the main reason we could go so far!"

"And that's exactly why they feared me."

Three magic circles appeared from nowhere, and three demons emerged.

"Do you really think they could hail a monster as a hero?"

Even though I wanted to deny it, something held me back.

Why can I not speak?!

With a snap of Laro's fingers, the demons melted into nothing.

"It's not your fault. I know this power is detestable."

I could no longer maintain eye contact with him.

"And yet, only one person accepted me for who I am… No, for who I *was*."

My eyes were drawn to the grave in front of me.

"And it's because of me that she—"

"You're wrong!"

Only after he had said those words was I able to react.

"Your sister died smiling! She…didn't despise anyone, and she would surely want you to be happy!"

"What could you ever know about her?!"

Laro's voice was so forceful that it made me shudder.

"How much time do you think I spent with her? Do you have any idea how I felt when she died with that smile?! How much I love—"

His ranting stopped. I knew what he meant.

But I had to refute his words.

"I'm sure she loved this country until the very end."

Laro gave no response. A few seconds passed before I heard his faint voice.

"So you're determined to get in my way…?"

Huh?

Without giving me any time to react, Laro continued in a voice filled with anger.

"Do you think you know my sister better than I do?!"

"I didn't mean it like that! I just—"

"Then prove it to me!"

Pointing at his chest, he spoke firmly:

"I abandoned my humanity to become a demon; in doing so, I obtained a body capable of withstanding all contracts made with them. But there are some things that even I cannot change."

I had no idea where he was taking this conversation…

"Come on; I won't resist. If you say my sister loved this country, then *I*, the one who is trying to destroy it, am in the wrong!"

…no, I *did* know what he meant, but I couldn't accept it. If I did as he wished, I would *also* lose the person who was standing before my very eyes.

He approached me step by step.

"Kill me."

I was paralyzed by the pressure that he radiated with these two simple words.

From the tone of his voice, I could sense his loneliness, his distrust of me, and the depth of his despair. The person I once knew had changed completely, both from without and from within. Nauseated, I could no longer think straight.

Seeing no reaction from me, he turned around.

"Just as I thought… You see only the reality that suits you."

His figure slowly shrank into the distance…

"The next time we meet will be the last."

…and faded into the dark of night.

Once Laro was no longer in my field of vision, my body could finally move again.

I looked at his sister's grave and reflected on the argument that we had just had. I had no doubts as to what his last sentence meant.

The next time we meet, one of us will die.

I closed my eyes and spoke to the wind:

"What should I do?"

I slowly opened my eyes, clutching for anything that could help.

"Please… Fina, tell me…"

I did not find any answers. I could only retrace my steps and tell the other Guardian Spirits what had happened.

A few days later, we clashed on the battlefield. After a grueling confrontation, Laro and I were isolated from the rest.

The other Guardian Spirits lacked strength and had all been knocked unconscious. The rain was quickly draining the warmth from everyone's body, and had the fight not ended as soon as possible, my companions would have fallen to hypothermia.

"Come on!"

With the melancholy eyes from before, he pointed at his chest.

"This will be your last chance!"

He wasn't going to attack. And yet… I—

"As expected of a fool."

His tone had suddenly changed. Sensing my hesitation, Laro threw me to the ground. I couldn't say anything.

"How weak you creatures are."

There was nothing that I could do.

"Hesitating at the sight of a pathetic human…"

At that statement, I looked up at *it*.

"What…did you just say…?"

Laro…no, something that resembled him only in appearance, looked down at me with an amused expression.

"It would seem that you knew this human…but that is of no importance. *He is already dead.*"

I didn't want to believe it.

"Laro…is dead?"

The being before me nodded.

"Correct. His body bore so many contracts that it is a miracle that he survived until now. In the end, however, he collapsed."

I clenched my jaws.

"…When…?"

"Perhaps a few days ago? It seems that after a *particular* meeting, his sanity went awry."

I didn't know what to do. Its innuendo was all too obvious.

"Did I…do something wrong…?"

That creature's expression lit up.

"Incorrect. You did something right…*for me!*"

"AAAAAAHHHHHHHHHHHHHHH!!!!!!!!!!!!!!"

The creature's answer tore my heart in two.

Maybe I was deaf with despair, but I didn't hear any scorn from the creature. It was gazing at me with an unreadable expression on its face.

"That man was right."

Ignoring my inability to give it attention, the creature resumed its monologue.

"After being betrayed by your own country, it is right to seek revenge. However, something was tormenting him: *his fool of a sister.*"

My heart skipped a beat.

"Even though his sister was killed by her own country, that man still tried to convince himself that he was wrong. I can only laugh at his foolishness!"

I was seething.

"He thought that maybe his sister was right. That this country was beautiful. That there could be another path. What utter nonsense, as befits a fool!"

'Fool?!'

Unbeknownst to me, I stood up despite my lack of energy. The creature said nothing.

"…Take back what you said…"

It shrugged its shoulders to show its disappointment.

"One was a *fool*, and the other was a bigger *fool*. *Foolishness* must have flowed in their veins."

Its claws sank into my scales.

"They were *fools* to love this country. They were *fools* to fight, and like *fools* they died."

I couldn't hold myself back anymore.

"That man's desperation was truly pathetic. He even tried to find salvation by visiting his sister's grave. Such is the nature of their foolishness."

I cast my most powerful spell and focused it so that it would surely hit *its* heart.

"You don't have any right to talk about them like that!"

The creature summoned innumerable magic circles. *It* would surely have parried my attack. And yet…

The circles broke. The magic bullet hit *it* right in the middle. *Its* figure was disappearing. I could not understand what was happening, but I saw one thing.

He—was smiling.

The next moment, Laro's body disintegrated and faded into the wind. As if announcing the end of the battle, the weather cleared up, causing sunlight to illuminate the place where he had just stood.

Neither his body nor his ashes could be seen. He was gone.

Upon news of Laro's death, Minnesa quickly retreated behind the borders that had been established before the war of the two kingdoms. Since their main force had disappeared and they knew that they had no chance of victory, they chose to sign a new armistice to prevent further loss of life. What happened next *is* written in the history books, but there is a small part that only a few people know.

After the conflict, the Guardian Spirits were suspected of and charged with the research of forbidden spells relating to the origin of magic and with the resurrection of a particular demon. Their plans were thwarted, and they were sealed. However, since the people of the kingdom regarded them as saviors and the kingdom feared that without them, neighboring countries would invade, it granted restricted freedom to each of them.

Freedom within a certain, purpose-built facility—Solset Magic Academy.

✳✳✳

"So… Why the long story?"

After listening to my tale of the past, Simon was puzzled. Marie, on the other hand, was smiling as if she had already figured it out. Nevertheless, she told me with her eyes to explain it.

"I'm afraid that you'll end up like those two…"

For me, it was a rather complicated matter; since their situation was similar, I feared the worst case. Even so, their answers were completely unexpected.

"Basically, I'll become the next Demon King?"

"And I'll end up dying?"

I didn't know what to say; their tone of voice was not serious at all. I was furious.

"I am—"

""We know.""

They stopped my complaint at the same time, before I could even make it.

"I know that I'll probably be the reason for my sister's death."

"And I know that I will one day die to protect my brother."

I had no words; they already knew what fate would await them if they continued along this path.

"Then—"

""But…""

Their gaze, full of determination, was about to answer my fear.

"My sister needs me."

"And my brother relies on me."

Neither sibling needed to look at the other before responding.

"Even though we know this will lead to our deaths…"

"…we have already accepted our fate."

I was stunned; I could not believe their resolve. Even before hearing my tale, they had known all along what would befall them in the future, yet despite that, they were not afraid.

Although I respected their determination, there was something that absolutely annoyed me. It wasn't altruism—quite the opposite, in fact.

I don't want to see that *scene again.*

Before I could say anything, Simon turned around.

"Also, it's enough if I can protect my sister."

He began walking forward, never looking back.

"This is *my one true purpose.*"

At that instant, I doubted my eyes—Simon's figure overlapped with that of a man I knew all too well.

A slender hand gently patted my head.

"Thank you for worrying about my brother."

Huh?

Something *really* was wrong with my vision. I was still seeing a certain pair who were no longer of this world.

"You don't need to punish yourself anymore."

I couldn't understand Marie's words.

"You've always been tormented by his final smile, haven't you?"

...I couldn't deny it. After making all those speeches about what his sister wanted, I couldn't trust myself anymore.

"In my opinion, you were right."

I looked directly into her eyes, which were full of sincerity.

"*I'm sure she loved this country until the end.* And not only Fina—Laro too."

My vision was becoming blurry.

"Inside, he knew you were right, and that's why he died smiling. He was happy that you stopped him."

Why...?

I did nothing but watch you die.

But the girl in front of me said nothing. She smiled, continuing to move her hand as if she wanted to wipe away my pain.

"Since you depicted me as his sister, I'll tell you this in her place."

No, please don't say that.

I was unsure whether I would be able to restrain myself.

"Thank you."

At that moment, her figure overlapped entirely with an image of that girl who was so lively and radiant.

"…Why are you…thanking me?"

I was not expecting an answer. The tears that fell from my face washed away my regrets as I accepted those two meaningful words.

***

"Marie, come here for a moment!"

Realizing that the discussion was over, Simon called Marie, who joined him shortly afterward.

"I need your help. There's one last thing that I must do before leaving the academy."

Leaving…the academy?

What was he saying?!

"Sure."

"One moment…"

Stunned, I was a bit late to interrupt their conversation:

"Are you going to leave the academy…?"

"That is correct."

There was no hesitation in his voice.

"…Why…?"

But deep down, I already knew the answer.

"Because I am a demon. What other reason could there be?"

I didn't know how to respond. No matter where you asked, demons were feared creatures, and Gilar was no exception.

"You're going to abandon your sister just like that…?"

"What are you saying? We'll leave together, of course!"

I couldn't understand what *she* was saying.

"As much as it pains me to separate my sister from the academy, she will follow me wherever I go."

It was then that I remembered the talk that we had had shortly after defeating my alter ego.

***

"Your wounds…!"

Although Simon had received multiple hits during the fight, there were no traces of injury anywhere on his body. His movements were also entirely regular; it was as if the sounds of bones shattering during the battle had all been nothing but illusions.

"No matter how physically injured I may be, my regeneration is so fast that it won't even leave any scars."

He wasn't lying. All of the bleeding had stopped, and no parts of his body looked damaged. The only evidence of the battle that remained was the blood that caked his uniform.

Suddenly, a magic circle appeared at Simon's feet, illuminating and enveloping him. He did not seem surprised, though, and remained still. When the glow faded, his uniform sparkled like new. Simon turned to face his sister, who was smiling peacefully.

"Thank you, Marie."

"You're welcome."

I just couldn't keep up with these two…

At that moment, I remembered to ask the most important thing:

"If you're so strong, why didn't you stand up to Phillip in your first duel?"

Eyes notwithstanding, the *spell* that he had used to summon his swords was unrelated to being a demon…if peculiar.

"I don't like to attract attention, and also…"

Both Simon and Marie looked down.

"…I cannot make them without using these eyes."

A sword appeared from thin air.

"Since I am of mixed blood, I need to see the spell's code to get the shape that I want."

The sword disappeared.

"Because of these eyes… No, because of my existence, my magic circuit is completely irregular, and I cannot control my spells in the traditional way."

I remembered his first duel against Phillip.

"But didn't you summon a golem?"

Simon had a bitter expression on his face.

"…Could you really call that a *spell*?"

Of course, the size and power were mediocre, but the summoning itself…

"…It took me about five years to get enough control of my magic circuit to do that."

"Five…years…"

It was then that I understood the reason for his dejection. After five years of training, a result like that was more than unsatisfactory. Weak attack, fragile armor, and a time limit…

"One moment… In that case, what was the real cause of that explosion that occurred at the end of the duel?"

Now that I knew the extent of Simon's actual magic reserves, the issue was not *how* it happened but *why*. And also…

"Why is it that you slept for two entire days after that duel, and yet now you're more than energetic?"

It was Marie who answered:

"I'm pretty sure my brother was looking for a draw."

"A draw?"

I glanced at Simon for confirmation; he nodded.

"The only way to keep you from getting what you wanted without displaying my true ability was to get a draw."

"He only fainted because he tried too hard to restrain his magic."

"Restrain?"

"Simon's spells are too powerful because he's…a demon, and in order to keep his spells from going out of control, he must make an effort to restrain his magical power."

"For this reason, I used the first few minutes of the duel to disperse as much magic as I could, but something unexpected occurred."

Simon's gaze briefly rested on Phillip, who was still unconscious.

"Without being able to use these eyes of mine, I was too late to discover the true magical composition of his golems."

"The fact that they have a thicker layer on the surface and are hollow on the inside?"

"Yes. If I had tried to force a draw, defeating that golem would still have been possible. However…I would have had to blow up part of the arena as well, so it took me longer to create a weak spot that did not require as much power."

The idea that Simon could destroy the building while hundreds of students were inside made me shudder.

"But in doing so, he had to push himself beyond his limits. The result is as you saw."

"…Indeed. But how is this related to the question of him now being able to use an immense amount of magic without any drawbacks?"

"Because that's his normal amount, which he can use without any restrictions."

That much?!

That is what I nearly blurted out before I managed to hold my shock back. I am quite confident in my evaluation when I say that every single sword that he created in the previous fight had the same power as one of my alter ego's bullets, to say nothing of the amount of magic that cloaked his body.

"So why did you use a catalyst to cast that magic circle?"

"Do you mean this?"

"I have one too."

Both Simon and Marie showed me their catalysts. Although they were different, the material and design of the objects showed that they had been forged by the same craftsman.

"These were gifts…"

Simon stopped talking. Marie completed his sentence in a faint whisper.

"…from when we were children."

I was finally beginning to understand.

"You mean that you were intentionally using an unsuitable catalyst in order to disperse your magical power, instead of focusing it?"

Simon nodded, but something was strange…

"Why are you doing the same thing?"

I directed this question toward Marie.

"These catalysts are special; they can be modified as many times as you want, but it takes almost half a day to fine-tune them."

"Also… These catalysts represent bad memories."

Simon looked away; to my surprise, Marie did the same. I looked back to see Simon's expression of deep regret.

"…That's why I don't want to use spells any more than necessary."

The unstated conclusion was obvious:

Because it would make it obvious that I'm a monster.

His gaze just then reminded me of a story of the past. And it was at that moment that I began to tell them of the origin of the Demon King.

✳✳✳

Thinking back on that discussion, I finally realized it—the true reason for which Simon did not want to use his power. It wasn't because he feared the attention; it was a simpler reason, and his expression now confirmed my theory.

"Simon Anion… I will reveal to no one that you are a demon."

Hearing my words, the siblings' expressions were astonished.

"How come…?"

It was Marie who asked why.

"I witnessed your brother's *determination*. I will no longer force Simon to become my academic representative."

They did not know what to say; it was no wonder, since I had previously been so insistent. But I was telling the truth.

"Then, Phillip—"

"No."

I interrupted Simon.

"After all the things that he has done, he cannot become an academic representative. In fact, he shall be punished severely."

Neither of them knew what to say.

"That's why I promise—"

My eyes met Simon's.

"—I swear on my name and on my very being that I will not reveal your true identity to anyone until you yourself want to…"

Sensing my sincerity, Simon thought deeply about the matter.

"…and neither of you will have to leave the academy."

Suddenly, Simon's face became beet red. It seemed that Marie didn't realize why her brother was doing all this.

"All right!"

He turned quickly to face me, his excitement changing to a look of annoyance.

"…But I'm not doing this for the reason you think!"

At his reaction, I smiled genuinely.

Like him, *he acts only for his sister's sake…*

Though they were different people, it was starting to become believable that the person in front of me was Laro's heir.

"…Wait for me here. I'll be right back."

"All right."

With that quick exchange, Simon proceeded to return to the academy. Only Marie and I remained.

"What will the two of you do now, Marie?"

She didn't have anything to hide.

"Save this cave—that is what my brother and I will do."

At first, I did not understand what she meant, but I soon remembered what Simon had said when he was exploring the maze. After a short pause, Marie spoke:

"Those three rules I imposed on him might seem to be enforced…"

This sudden change of topic left me bewildered.

"…but they aren't. In truth, my brother would like to save *everyone*."

Her expression both shone with pride and harbored an immense sadness.

"That's why I brought him to this academy."

She turned around so that I would not see her face.

"Chatting in class, making friends, and finding something that he could truly dedicate himself to… As trivial as it was, I wanted him to find something for himself."

It was then that her voice dropped to a whisper:

"And in doing so, maybe he could finally be free of me."

I didn't say anything; I *couldn't* say anything. All I could do was look up at the ceiling and admire the plants as they continued to give off a soft light.

They were truly stunning, but there was no one to admire them. For over two centuries, their only audience had been a pathetic creature that had lost its way. Yet, they had continued, undaunted, to give light to their surroundings.

I, too, had to start shining for someone. To not allow these two to stray down the wrong path. But how could I achieve that?

I looked down and saw Phillip, who was still unconscious.

That was the worst student I could ever have chosen as my representative.

I reflected on everything that had happened over the last few years—not only because of Phillip but also because of the other Earth representatives. I knew that I had to do something. Yet, somewhere deep down, I still wanted Simon to become my representative.

But I already said that I would not force him, no?

At that moment, I remembered the main cause of all of my problems; just thinking about it made my head hurt. And yet, just like that, I had a brilliant idea.

I said I wouldn't force him anymore, but what if he wants to?

The thought of using the source of all of my nightmares to get the result that I wanted was repulsive to me…but a part of me was glad that such a method existed at all.

But what excuse can I give?

I looked again at the figure of Phillip. I didn't know why, but I thought that he could give me an answer. It's like I had a *hunch*.

At that moment, a second stroke of genius came to me.

Using *that* excuse, I could put my plan into motion.

My body was so full of energy that it was as if the last two hundred years had never occurred at all.

"It's time to set the stage—so that this time, I won't have any regrets!"

Jubilant, I returned to the academy.

014: Epilogue

"…for this reason, Phillip Royals has been expelled from the academy."

All the students who were gathered in the main hall started whispering.

"Hey, is he telling the truth?"

"Would Phillip really lose control and nearly destroy the academy?"

"Isn't this another one of his ploys to appoint Simon as the Earth representative?"

"Silence!"

At my command, all students stopped talking.

If anything, expulsion was an extremely lenient punishment given the circumstances. Only my good mood allowed him to get away with such a light penalty.

"A few days ago, did you not feel strong quakes that could have destroyed even the strongest building?"

No one objected.

I was right in the epicenter to assist and the cave—whose barrier-filled walls that were designed to keep my true body chained could not even be *scratched* by regular attacks— was absorbing the magic bullets. Despite this, Phillip's irresponsible actions had still created powerful tremors that could be felt even at the academy four hundred meters above our battlefield.

"The academy and its facilities are imbued with the magical power of all five Guardian Spirits and designed to withstand even the assault of an entire army. Despite this, Phillip's inability to control the power that he stole from me almost ended in a tragedy."

Now was the time for me to make full use of my narration abilities. While it was true that the *buildings* of the academy were protected by the Guardian Spirits in an attempt to consume our natural regeneration of magic particles, this did not apply to the ground.

Thus, it was truly a miracle that the academy did not sink. To prevent a leak of information and avoid panicking the students, concealing a part of the truth was a necessity. Naturally, only the Guardian Spirits and the headmaster knew about this, so we received no objections.

Now is the time to put my plan into action.

"The one who foiled this threat was Simon Anion!"

In that instant, the eyes of everyone in the assembly hall focused on that first-year student. His expression was irate; it seemed like I was going against what I had told him in the cave. He glared at me, clearly wanting to know what I was planning.

"His true strength is more than worthy of becoming the next Earth representative. This I guarantee as Guardian Spirit."

The audience buzzed, perplexed. Before Simon could open his mouth to object…

"That's why I will ask one last time."

The entire hall was rapt.

"Simon Anion, would you like to become my representative?"

All eyes were on Simon. His eyes were closed.

Clenching his fists with determination, he opened his eyes.

"No."

Neither Simon nor I paid any attention to the students' whispers, and we continued our conversation to make the matter official.

"May I know why?"

Simon took a deep breath. He looked directly at me and loudly made his declaration:

"*Anyone* who wants to play at such a role is nothing but an idiot."

Simon's words caused more than a simple commotion. Everyone felt attacked by his scathing declaration, which was directed at *all* of the academic representatives—the most trusted figures in the academy.

"Such is the nature of their foolishness."

Though it had been more than two centuries, I remembered the words of a particular man. I had finally understood their true meaning: 'It is foolish to toil alone and bear all burdens for the sake of achieving your goal…*but it is even more foolish to allow regret to cloud your judgment and prevent you from finishing what you have started.'*

"Then, it is decided."

These two *humans* were very similar.

"I will no longer attempt to name Simon Anion as my representative."

Hearing my words, all students—Simon included—breathed a sigh of relief. And because of this, my plan had a chance of success.

"Since the other candidate, Phillip Royals, has been expelled, it would now fall on me to find another possible candidate. I have decided…"

The students chatted among themselves, presumably sharing their thoughts as to whom I could be talking about. With the most amused expression that a reptile like me could make, I declared with more excitement than I had felt in over two centuries:

"…that there will be no Earth representative this year."

The students were astonished. Faris could not contain their objections. It seemed that I would have to lend a helping hand.

"Do you think it easy to decide upon an academic representative?"

Since I was offering an explanation, a fleeting calm returned to the hall.

"Could you name another candidate besides Phillip Royals?"

No one answered. It was quite obvious: for all these years, the role of academic representative had been handed down by the previous year's representative. No one else had strived to compete with the 'chosen one.' Thus, no one could confidently suggest another candidate, much less choose one whom the majority of their element would trust.

"Since the one whom I wanted as my representative did not accept the position, I have no choice but to make this decision."

All eyes were focused on Simon once more.

"If you truly desire a representative, you are more than welcome to expend as much effort as you wish on trying to convince him."

With that proclamation, I turned around and left the room. I did not listen to the students' chatter, but certainly, Simon at the very least was cursing me to death. If anything, however, I was simply using the same strategy that he had—I was prepared to be hated if it meant achieving the result that I wanted.

Before I knew it, I was practically dancing with happiness at my success. As I walked down the hall, I saw a familiar figure: the headmaster of Solset.

"Sorry about that, Faris."

"A simple apology is nowhere near enough to make up for what you did... The situation was so bad that I could only delegate the cleanup to the other professors and hope for the best."

Seeing Faris's gloomy expression and sigh of resignation, I could only heartily chuckle at the thought that he had sneaked off in front of the entire student body. I continued talking:

"You'll at least do all of the paperwork necessary to keep Earth running smoothly, right?"

"...Did something good happen to you?"

Puzzled, I couldn't help but tilt my head.

"...Something good? What makes you say that?"

Faris let his gaze wander to the ceiling before returning it to my face.

"Mm... I'd say you're going back to doing things your own way?"

Silently reflecting on my past, I realized that my attitude was completely passive.

"Perhaps you're right."

I continued walking down the hall, but briefly turned my head to face Faris.

"I've finally found someone who can surprise me."

✳✳✳

"So… mind telling me what *really* happened, Simon?"

Rachael and I were on the academy's terrace. After finishing my studies in the astronomy room, I had met her outside the door, before accompanying her here. Since there were no buildings on the terrace to shield one from the elements, the wind was strong—but not strong enough to blow a person off the edge or prevent a conversation. If anything, it seemed that this was a perfect place to tell secrets, since no one could eavesdrop over the howl of the wind.

"Whatever could you mean?"

"I'm talking about what happened down there."

She pointed at the ground; she was definitely talking about what had happened a few days ago and Domizio's shocking announcement.

"Well, it's more or less what the Guardian Spirit of Earth said: Phillip lost control after becoming the Earth representative and almost destroyed the entire academy."

Rachael looked right at me, a serious expression in her eyes. Arms crossed, she stubbornly probed for an answer:

"But why did Phillip become the representative in the first place? Sure, he was strong, but I've heard that he wasn't able to pass the Guardian Spirit's final trial. And for that matter, if he was so strong, how was his rampage stopped?"

Sighing deeply, I asked a question of my own:

"Where are Mark and Lucas? Are they not with you?"

"I'm not always with them, and they know I need time to gather information."

"Does this mean that today your role is Informant Too Cute for—"

"Simon, don't change the topic."

Her expression did not change. It didn't seem like she would let it go so easily; she had the same look as *that time*. Because of that, I had to respond honestly, so I—

Rachael grabbed my uniform sleeve, preventing me from making the quick departure that I had planned.

This is not the first time, right?

"What are you hiding?"

"Many… Too many things."

Sensing my melancholy mood, she released her grip.

"Your sister was kidnapped. Right?"

I tried not to let my surprise show on my face, but Rachael already seemed entirely convinced.

"That's why the Guardian Spirit of Earth was forced to appoint Phillip as representative even though he didn't want to. But something went wrong with Phillip's plans—somehow, he was stopped, and then he was expelled."

I stayed silent.

"I want your opinion on this very rough reconstruction of mine."

I could no longer maintain my poker face.

"W-what is it, Simon? Why are you grinning?"

"It's…nothing."

Even though she could have fabricated a better story to corner me, she had simply asked for my impression of her 'very rough reconstruction.' Despite her line of questioning being quite intrusive, it didn't seem pushy at all.

She remembered my words.

Faced with this, I had no choice but to tell her the truth.

"It was yours truly who forced the Guardian Spirit to appoint Phillip as his representative, and the same yours truly who forced Phillip to lose control. 'Who defeated Phillip?' you might ask? Why, it was none other than…yours truly!"

Naturally, my playful tone was deliberate. Rachael's expression leaked pure surprise, and it took her a few seconds to recover.

"I see… So that's what happened…"

Now *I* was surprised.

"…You…believe me?"

Rachael smiled sweetly.

"The job of an informant is to trust her sources. Also…"

Rachael gazed wistfully at the sunset before meeting my eyes again.

"…we're friends, aren't we?"

I was caught off guard.

"I won't ask what *really* happened, but I want to trust you."

My heart leaped.

Rachael walked toward the terrace door. Once she was halfway there, I asked her one last question:

"Why do you…trust me?"

"Why do I trust you, huh…"

She turned around and walked until she was in front of me once more.

"Because I'm everyone's favorite secret informant!"

After her trademark gesture of putting on an invisible pair of glasses, she lowered her voice.

"…And also, you two have the nicest expressions I've ever seen."

You two*, huh…*

That meant—

"I don't want to suspect anyone anymore."

I completely understood what she just said, but…

"…You shouldn't trust me."

"Well that's just too bad, isn't it?"

The evening hue gave Rachael a slightly more mature aura than usual. As she leaned on the railing, her scarlet eyes stared directly at me as if observing my very soul. Within them, I could see my own reflection gently enveloped by her warm gaze amidst the twilight.

"Because I'm the same as you. I, too, do not so easily forget the favors of others."

Showing a mischievous smile, she pointed at a particular object on my belt.

"You can call it *my foolishness*."

Leaving me with those words, she exited the terrace like a gust of wind.

∗∗∗

"Because I'm the same as you. I, too, do not so easily forget the favors of others."

"You can call it my foolishness."

As I walked home, my mind raced.

She didn't need a confirmation of anything—she was testing me.

Her parting words were the only proof I needed; I didn't know what, but she clearly knew *something* about what had happened underground and the events that followed.

I held up the object that I was carrying on my belt. It was a pocket watch with a metal lid that displayed the figure of a golden butterfly. Unlike the previous one, however, it featured a single precious gemstone at its center. More importantly…

The hands inside it—they moved.

∗∗∗

"Fix this pocket watch?"

It was the very day of Domizio's shocking announcement—two hours before it, in fact.

"That is correct. I want you to go to the four other Elemental Sanctuaries and convince their respective Guardian Spirits to bestow their blessings upon this pocket watch. At the moment, it has no magical power and serves only to keep the time."

Looking at the timepiece on the headmaster's office table, I asked the obvious question:

"But didn't I destroy it?"

"Well… What you destroyed *was* the original, but I mainly used it to connect the flow of my magic with that of my representative; although that was theoretically not its main purpose, the academy would be in trouble if such an item did not exist."

"…Why should I help you?"

At that moment, I noticed a slight change in his expression.

Looks like I'm getting better at reading that lizard's emotions.

"Tell me; who exactly was it that asked me not to reveal the fact that a certain person was kidnapped?"

I had no words. I *had* asked Domizio to keep quiet about the kidnapping, in order to prevent my sister from being bothered by her classmates and professors.

I never imagined that I would be blackmailed like this…

"…All right…"

"Well, it's settled, then."

Using his snout, he tossed the timepiece in my direction; I caught it casually.

"You shall go to the four other Elemental Sanctuaries, with their respective academic representatives as your guides."

Hearing those words, I began to protest:

"Guides? You know very well that I don't need any!"

"Well, you know what they say… 'There are those who do not wish for their homes to be visited by strangers.'"

I initially agreed with him—but then remembered that he wasn't a human being.

"These are sanctuaries, are they not? Besides, it's *your* request."

Although he appeared to understand my motivations, Domizio swept away all of my objections just like he did the first time.

"Article 4, Paragraph 2: Areas restricted by element may be accessed by students of other elements only if they are accompanied by at least one (1) Suitably Qualified Member of the correct element…"

Ah!

I recalled what I had discussed with my sister a few days ago—the five Elemental Sanctuaries were the most heavily restricted locations of the academy, with only the academic representatives permitted to enter them.

"…Suitably Qualified Members include but are not limited to—"

"Okay, I get it! …What are you planning?"

To my chagrin, I was still unable to read minds, but it was evident that this creature was up to something.

"…Nothing exceptional…"

A blatant lie.

"…Got it."

Just before I left the room, I heard one last comment from that meddling lizard:

"Have fun! *Both you and the girls.*"

✳✳✳

Just remembering that talk made my morale plummet. That last comment of his was especially disturbing.

"…Did he *really* fight to change the reputation of Earth…?"

I remembered that one of the points that he despised was that the previous Earth representatives had all been womanizers…and now, he was deliberately trying to play matchmaker…?

What the hell is he thinking?!

I stared at the brooch on my uniform collar. I had tried to give it back to him, but he didn't seem to want it back.

"Call it an abundance of caution."

It's more likely to be destroyed before I use it…

I resisted the temptation to use it now to tell him *exactly* what I thought and arrived home.

"I'm back."

"…Welcome home!"

My sister was late to welcome me despite hearing my greeting, but when I saw her smile, all negative thoughts immediately disappeared from my mind.

When I'm at home, I don't need to think about anything else.

But suddenly my oasis shattered like a mirage.

"We have guests today. They're in in the living room."

"…Huh?"

There were four extra pairs of shoes at the door.

Girls' shoes.

Don't tell me…

I had a hunch as to how this would turn out…but I went to check the living room anyway. Four girls were sitting around the table, enjoying shortcakes that they had probably brought themselves and some tea that my sister had made. Clockwise from my left, they were:

A girl with long loose red hair. With a haughty aura about her, she seemed like she would be hard to get along with.

A girl with long blue hair held together with a wooden hairpin. With a peaceful aura about her, she seemed somewhat timid.

A girl with long black hair tied back in a ponytail. With an imposing aura about her, she seemed diligent.

A girl with short wavy yellow hair. With a carefree aura about her, she seemed easygoing.

If this is what I think it is…

The girl with the red hair stood up.

"You are Simon Anion, yes?"

Without even waiting for me to confirm her guess, she started the introductions.

"We are the four academic representatives of Solset Magic Academy."

It looked like my peaceful life would have to wait for a while yet.

Bonus

[**Author**] And here's the end-of-volume drama you've all been waiting for!

[**Fire Girl**] Wait just one moment!

[**Author**] ?

[**Fire Girl**] Don't play dumb! How dare you not introduce us before finishing this volume?!

[**Water Girl**] …Lucy, please calm down for a minute…

[**Lightning Girl**] I think you should like…totally let the author tell the story at his own pace, okay~?

[**Lucy**] But it took that…*snail* a year to write not even one hundred pages!

[**Author**] Urgh!

[**Lucy**] Who knows how much longer it will be before we get to appear!

[**Wind Girl**] You should be the least worried of all of us.

[**Lucy**] Huh?!

[**Wind Girl**] According to the script, it is you who will be the heroine of the next volume.

[**Water Girl**] …That's right…I think.

[**Lightning Girl**] Oh well, looks like I'm last~

[**Author, Lucy**] Hey, where did you get those scripts?!

[**Simon**] I found them in a desk drawer. It was locked.

[**Author**] Then you shouldn't have opened it!

[**Marie**] Anyway, setting aside the plot, which seems like a carbon copy of a certain series with an irregular, flawed older brother and an honor roll, flawless younger sister… The descriptions are really weak.

[**Author**] Um…

[**Wind Girl**] Furthermore, the antagonists often seem to appear solely to propel the plot forward.

[**Author**] Argh!

[**Simon**] And I'm already so strong that I can't get upgrades anymore. Who do you expect me to fight in order to hold our dear readers' attention?

[**Author**] *dies*

[**Water Girl**] Ah, Author! …Please pull yourself together!

[Lightning Girl] You totally have to write our story before you die~!

[Marie] That's right. I don't want this story to have a *bad* end.

[Simon] …So you've already read the ending…

[Author] *comes back to life* Hey! You shouldn't read that part!!!

[Marie] Don't worry about it; I'm fine with an ending like that. Then…

[Lucy] …Just why are you staring at me?

[Marie] No reason… I can't wait to see you in action, my dear.

[Lucy] Why are you being so familiar?!

[Wind Girl] You would do well to feel that way, given the amount of humiliation that awaits you.

[Lucy] Hey, give me those scripts! I demand to know what will happen to me!

[Lightning Girl] No can do~

[Lucy] Nives, you're my last hope! You're on my side, right? Right?!

[Nives] …Um…good luck!

[Lucy] You traitor!

[Simon] I can't wait to tea—…cooperate with you.

[Lucy] You were going to say 'tease,' weren't you?!

[Simon] I wonder…

[Lucy] I'm surrounded by enemies!

[Author] Look forward to the next volume!

Author's Afterword

Everybody, welcome to my personal corner (A.K.A. ranting room)!

For years, I've been known as chrnomaker, a wannabe writer that has always been charmed by Japanese culture.

I started writing stories in my second grade of high school (around 15 years ago) and this is the first time I've tried to publish something.

I've written a few things and I have in my mind a lot more, but I want to focus on one series at a time.

One True Purpose is the second series that I've written at least one volume of and it was written around 10 years ago.

It's funny that even after so much time, the events of the story are still fresh and not outdated…well, at least I hope so.

As you might have seen, my native language is Italian and not English and these author's notes are different from *Un Solo Obiettivo*, the Italian version of *One True Purpose*.

Not only that, a few other minor differences are present and won't be changed between the two versions.

The main reason is because the English version is under the mighty management of the editor, teacup2also.

As for our encounter, it was inside the tall grass of Discord.

I didn't even use a P**é Ball; he literally joined my party by himself!

That's when I realized that the English version I translated myself was utter trash lol.

Polishing and revising the whole thing…this project took 5 months to be finished.

It needs to be said that it was a hellish journey, especially the last few days of proofreading, but at last it's finally published!

The illustrator, uiyoyo199, was scouted by me on an art site.

His art is top-notch, but we had a ton of issues with communication, and often we made silly mistakes about what to draw.

I'm really moved by his trust in my work and I hope this series will bring him much more fame.

Fun fact: I turned down an actual publishing proposal in order to enter the global marketplace.

Feeling restricted by only a native marketplace, I really wanted to aim for an English release.

Doing so, I took on all spending for the illustrations, figured out how and where to publish, plus other minor things that I never realized were behind an actual published book.

It was stressful and a very selfish wish, but the end work is so beautiful that I might cry.

I'm very lucky to be supported by capable people and I really want to work hard so this series will see its proper end.

I pray you'll watch the journey of this series and give me reviews of my writing, as it is part of my mentality, my identity, and my life.

chrnomaker

June 2022

Editor's Afterword

Cordial salutations, dear readers! It is I, teacup2also, first-time editor! I first came across this work in late 2021, when the author promoted it on a certain online chatroom that I frequent. I decided to check it out on a whim and was immediately sold on the premise (indeed, I, too, enjoy a certain series about the…dramatic life that unfolds when two siblings enroll in a magic academy). However! The English writing was…well, it could have been better. For you see, dear readers, though our author here valiantly gave his all, translating into a language one is not fluent in is no trivial task. And that's where I came in! I enjoyed the story so much that I decided to offer to edit its English translation —an offer that was graciously accepted.

Through editing this book, I have learnt (Yep, that's right—everyone's favourite ~~secret informant~~ editor is Bri'ish…ish and had to fight back tears every time he spelt colour the American way, innit?) a lot, and I hope to keep on learning as I continue to edit the rest of the series! As for my most interesting story from the editing process, that would have to be the time that I misread the author's intentions and accidentally made the interlude too…*anime*. If you know, you know.

Anyway, teacup2also out!

P.S. [REDACTED] best girl! Wait, just what do you think you're doing with that sword? No! Don't stare at me with those ey—

teacup2also

June 2022

Illustrator's Afterword

Thank you to all of our readers. This is a project that I've been working on for the past six months. It's also about learning new things from this work for me. Have a good time with this novel's plot.

uiyoyo199

December 2021

Hey, you make me feel like an idiot for writing so much for my afterword!

chrnomaker

December 2021

Follow us on social media!

Author

Twitter: @chrnomaker
Instagram: chrnomaker

Illustrator

Twitter @uiyoyo199

Use **#OTPurpose** hashtag to discuss the series, please!